He turned in her direction and g... trademark Beau McLintock smile. "Anything else?"

"Yes." Jess wanted to be immune from that smile, unaffected by the heat simmering in his eyes. Instead, her skin flushed and she struggled to take in air. *Concentrate.* "Do you want to do it?" Damn it, she sounded like a breathless teenager.

His smile morphed into a sexy grin. "Anytime you want, sweet lady."

Whoops. Miscommunication. Heart hammering, she fought the urge to grab him. "I was…" She gulped. "I was talking about who would make the announcement to your family."

His tone turned brisk. "I knew that's what you meant."

"No, you didn't. Your pupils dilated."

"You can't tell in this light."

"I can so." She took a shaky breath. "I can see your face in the glow from that tree."

"My *sweet* face?" He'd shifted back to seductive mode, murmuring the words and leaning toward her, bringing with him the scent of pine and aroused male.

"Don't you dare kiss me."

His voice lowered another notch. "You want me to."

HAVING THE
COWBOY'S BABY

ROWDY RANCH

Vicki Lewis Thompson

Ocean Dance Press

HAVING THE COWBOY'S BABY
© 2022 Vicki Lewis Thompson

ISBN: 978-1-63803-953-2

Ocean Dance Press LLC
PO Box 69901
Oro Valley, AZ 85737

This is a work of fiction. Any resemblance to
actual persons, living or dead, business
establishments, events, or locales is entirely
coincidental.

Visit the author's website at
VickiLewisThompson.com

Want more cowboys? Check out these other titles by Vicki Lewis Thompson

The Buckskin Brotherhood

Sweet-Talking Cowboy
Big-Hearted Cowboy
Baby-Daddy Cowboy
True-Blue Cowboy
Strong-Willed Cowboy
Secret-Santa Cowboy
Stand-Up Cowboy
Single-Dad Cowboy
Marriage-Minded Cowboy
Gift-Giving Cowboy

The McGavin Brothers

A Cowboy's Strength
A Cowboy's Honor
A Cowboy's Return
A Cowboy's Heart
A Cowboy's Courage
A Cowboy's Christmas
A Cowboy's Kiss
A Cowboy's Luck
A Cowboy's Charm
A Cowboy's Challenge
A Cowboy's Baby
A Cowboy's Holiday
A Cowboy's Choice
A Cowboy's Worth
A Cowboy's Destiny
A Cowboy's Secret
A Cowboy's Homecoming

Sons of Chance

1

Beau McLintock dug a starting line in the dead grass with the toe of his boot. "Ready to race, guys?"

Slim, an all-black pot-bellied pig, trotted behind the line and dropped his haunches to the frozen ground. Pickens, his black and white little brother, squared up beside him and sat, quivering with eagerness. The race always topped off their late afternoon exercise routine, and Pickens loved it the most, even though he continued to lose.

"Stay." Beau added the hand signal out of habit. They didn't need it. Those pigs were so damned smart. Smarter than any of the horses. Probably smarter than his mom's collie, Sam. His mom would likely debate him on the subject, though.

Slim and Pickens held their position as he walked to the far side of the fenced enclosure, the grass crackling under his boots. Today was almost warm, unseasonably so for the first week in February. Wouldn't last. This was Montana, after all.

Nobody was around, but Beau took the role of announcer, anyway. The pigs liked it better when he ramped up the drama. Curling his fist into a make-believe microphone, he injected tense anticipation into his voice. "And they're in the starting gate. A hush falls over the crowd. Waiting for the bell... *ding,* they're off!"

The pigs galloped toward him, short legs pumping, looking like motorized duffle bags.

"Slim takes the lead, but Pickens won't be denied! He makes his move *aaaand* it's Pickens in the lead! But Slim overtakes him! They're neck-and-neck and it's Pickens by a snout!" Laughing, he dug in his pocket and passed out treats as the pigs wagged their tails like crazy. "Good boys." He crouched down to give them both head rubs.

They flopped and rolled so he could scratch their bellies, too. "Pickens, you did it, son! Knew you could. Slim, you gotta bring your A-game next time. Your little brother is—"

The distant purr of an engine grew louder. Sounded more like an SUV than a truck heading down the dirt road. His family drove trucks. What if it was...? Nah, couldn't be.

But it was. The flash of deep blue through the pines used to fill him with joy. He gulped.

Against all odds, Jessica Hartmann was about to set foot on Rowdy Ranch property. On Christmas Eve, she'd vowed never to do that again. Folks must be ice-skating in hell.

When he rose to his feet, Slim and Pickens scrambled up, tails wagging. Those pigs loved company almost as much as they loved racing.

The engine stopped. A door opened. It closed with a normal thump instead of a loud crack. That was a good sign, right?

He sucked in a breath. "I'm out back, Jess!"

"Figured!" She came around the side of the cabin, her green wool coat buttoned up to her chin, her red hair tucked under a white stocking cap. She hadn't slammed the car door, but judging from her tense expression, she wasn't pleased to be here.

"This is unexpected." Heart in his throat, he walked quickly over to the mesh gate.

"I'm sure it is." Anxiety filled her green eyes. She shoved her hands into her coat pockets and hunched her shoulders. Yeah, not pleased *at all.*

Slipping out of the enclosure a step ahead of the pigs, he latched the gate. Jess clearly wasn't in a pig-petting mood. "What's up?"

"You're not gonna believe this."

"I might." Hard to breathe, this close to her. But passing out wasn't an option, so he gave it his best shot. "Pickens just beat Slim in the big race. And you're standing here. Surprises come in threes."

She frowned. "I thought it was bad luck that comes in threes."

"Surprises, too."

"Alrighty, then. Here's number three. I'm pregnant."

He snorted in disbelief. "Leave the bad jokes to me, okay?"

"I'm not joking."

His stomach bottomed out. No, it couldn't be. He made mistakes, but not this kind. The timing, though…. Damn it, he'd used—

"I know what you're thinking, and I—"

"I buy the best." His ears buzzed. "I check the expiration dates. I—"

"I believe you." She glanced down, cleared her throat and looked up at him. "I might have the explanation."

"Super sperm?"

She blinked. For a split second she looked as if she might laugh. Or cry. Then she took a quick breath. "Midnight."

"Your *cat*? What the—"

"Over the weekend I deep-cleaned the house, trying to... come to grips with..." She made a vague gesture toward her flat stomach.

His attention went straight there. A baby. Dear God.

"Anyway, I found this." She held up a condom packet with teeth marks on the wrapper.

He fought dizziness. "I wouldn't have used a chewed one."

"Are you sure you'd notice?"

"Of course I'd notice." He said it fast and loud, desperate for it to be true. Except that first night he'd knocked a couple off the nightstand, then later had to retrieve one for a second round. Had Midnight been in the room? Hell, a pride of lions could have been in the room. He stared at her. Swallowed.

"You might need some time."

A baby. With a woman who was completely disgusted with him. "Time won't help."

"It's helped me. When I found out on Friday I was a total mess. But I've had the weekend to process this and today I'm... well, I'm here. I couldn't face that prospect two days ago."

He took a ragged breath. "Did you do the test yourself?"

"Yes. Then I went to Doc Bradley."

"So there's no doubt." The earth shifted beneath his feet.

"None. It's nobody's fault, but—"

"Is too. I'm pinning this on Midnight." There it was again. A blink, a gleam in her eyes. Probably a trick of the light.

Then she looked away. "Cats like things that crinkle."

Foiled by a black cat. And he'd thought they were friends.

"I, um, called your mom today." She faced him, chin lifted.

"You told her?"

"No. I asked if she could suggest a time when you'd be alone. She checked everybody's schedule and recommended pig-training time. But she'll want to know why I came to see you."

"I'll tell her. It's not like we can keep this a secret."

"Nope. But so far, you and Doc Bradley are the only ones with the info."

"You haven't told your dad?"

"You deserved to hear it first."

"Thank you." That was one of many reasons he'd fallen for Jess. She was a straight shooter. Then she'd shot him straight through the heart.

"You're taking it better than I expected. I braced myself for a bunch of wisecracks. You only made two."

"I can do better. I just need more time with the material."

"See? You can't resist. You can't take anything seriously. Not even—"

"Yes, I can. I just—"

"Never mind. We've had this argument. I'm gonna leave before we have it again." She turned and started back around the house.

"Wait. We have things to discuss."

"Later, Beau." She lengthened her stride. "I'll be in touch."

"Damn it, Jess." He went after her. Stopped himself. She wasn't ready to talk and neither was he. Turning back to the pig enclosure, he let himself in. The SUV's motor roared to life. Gone. Just like on Christmas Eve. Except now... *a baby.*

Slim and Pickens trotted over, looking for more treats. He pulled some out of his pocket, crouched down and handed them out. "Got a slight issue, guys." *An issue. Way to downplay it, dude.* "Correction. My life just changed, and it's never changing back."

A truck pulled up out front and a door opened and closed. He stood, grateful for whoever had stopped by. The pigs were great listeners, but he wanted advice. He exited the pen.

Sky, the oldest of his siblings and the closest in age, came around the side of the cabin. "Was that Jess I passed on the road?"

"That was Jess." Beau damn near threw his arms around his big brother. He couldn't have asked for a better advice giver than Sky.

"Social call?"

"Not hardly. She's…" The word stuck in his throat. He forced it out. "Pregnant."

Sky jerked backward as if he'd been hit with a sack of grain. "No."

"Evidently I used a condom her cat had chewed on."

"What?"

"I know it sounds crazy, but our first night together was a little… wild."

"That doesn't surprise me, but—"

"My condom supply ended up on the floor, and I used one without… I didn't think to check whether—"

"It had become a cat toy?"

"Exactly."

"Incredible." Sky nudged back his hat. "What're you going to do?"

"Besides drinking every beer in my fridge?"

"Besides that."

"Gotta tell mom."

"I'd advise staying sober until after you tell her."

"Where's the fun in that?"

Sky smiled. "Ah, good, you're back. You had me worried. For a minute, I thought I'd lost the crazy guy we all know and love."

"Not everyone loves that quality, bro."

Sky gazed at him. "Do you still love her?"

"I don't recall saying that I…" He avoided his brother's know-it-all look. Then he sighed. "Yeah, I do. But it's over."

"You sure?"

"If you'd heard her on Christmas Eve, you wouldn't have to ask the question. She is so done with me."

"Do you want to be a part of this kid's life?"

"Absolutely."

"Alrighty, then. First we'll tell mom and then—"

"We?"

"Sure. Penny texted me that she won't be back from UM for at least another hour, so I stopped by to grab a beer and discuss what to get Angie for her birthday."

"Right. That's coming up fast."

"Every Valentine's Day. Can't believe she'll be twenty-four."

"And this year she'll become an aunt."

Sky's eyes widened. "I didn't think of that. The rest of us will be uncles. Mom will be a grandma."

"How do you think she'll react?"

"Well, she loves babies." Sky shrugged, "That's in your favor."

"Yeah, but an accidental pregnancy? She's not gonna be thrilled."

"She might take it better than you think. I was an accident, and look how I turned out."

Beau grinned. "Trolling for compliments, bro?"

"Got one?"

He patted his coat pockets. "Thought I had one somewhere, but—"

"Anyway, after we break the news to her, we'll call a family meeting."

"Good idea. Then everybody gets the word at once."

"Plus we need help brainstorming."

"Brainstorming what? Jess holds all the cards."

"Not really. That baby's as much yours as hers."

"Technically, but—"

"If it's true she doesn't like you anymore, we need a plan."

2

Jess loved walking into the historic building that housed the *Wagon Train Sentinel*. An antique printing press stood on display in the lobby, testifying to the *Sentinel*'s proud tradition. It still had a faint ink smell.

Framed editions of the newspaper with headlines like *V-E Day!* and *Nixon Resigns!* decorated the walls. A glass display cabinet held old press passes, a black Speed Graphic camera with flash attachment, and a tattered reporter's notebook.

Her mom and dad had bought the struggling weekly before she was born. They'd revived it, using her mom's charm and business savvy to woo advertisers and her dad's talent for sparkling prose to attract readers.

She'd hung out here as a kid and had volunteered to cover high school sports her junior and senior year. Her primary motivation? Beau McLintock, the best athlete Wagon Train High ever had. The night she'd accidentally glimpsed him coming out of the locker room bare-chested and sweating had been the highlight of her brief sports writing career.

The *Sentinel* had thrived under her parents' management, and when her mom died five years ago, the paper had kept her dad going. It still would if she had anything to say about it.

Last summer he'd been ready to sell to a conglomerate. After talking him out of that bonehead decision, she'd resigned as anchorwoman at a Philadelphia TV station and moved home to work with him. Best decision ever. They'd had a blast.

She wasn't about to let this surprise pregnancy muck up their cozy dynamic. At least she had precedence on her side. Her parents had brought her to the office when she'd been weeks old. Her baby album had pictures to prove it.

Except she'd been planned, a joyful addition to the family. Instead of rejoicing when Doc Bradley had given her the news, she'd wanted to curse her rotten luck. Her dad would probably take it better than she had, but she didn't look forward to telling him.

As usual after closing time, he was alone in his office at the back typing madly on his computer. A self-taught typist, he used only his index fingers. And he could knock out a paragraph while she was still composing the opening sentence.

He glanced up with a happy smile and shoved his reading glasses to the top of his head. "This one's a winner, Jess. Kid saves dog a year ago, then today, dog saves kid. Can't get any better'n that."

"Dogs and kids." She returned his smile. "Terrific hook. It'll get picked up."

"I do believe it will. Damn, I love sharing stuff like this with you. Probably haven't thanked you enough for throwing in with me."

"Oh, yes, you have. Besides, I needed this as much as you did."

"Might be true. You have roses in your cheeks, as your mom used to say. Want to grab some dinner at the Fluffy Buffalo? I'll be through here in ten or fifteen."

"Sounds good." She left his office to give him space to put the finishing touches on a story that likely would go viral. He had the touch.

Perched on the edge of her vintage oak desk in the dimly-lit outer office, she took a steadying breath. The furniture had been here forever — two desks like hers and a couple of gray metal filing cabinets. They were ready for filing cabinet heaven, but her dad wouldn't hear of it. He rummaged through them now and then.

So did Monica Fulton, the veteran reporter they'd had on staff for thirty years. The other desk used to be her mom's. Joe Bianchi was the *Sentinel*'s ad manager now. Good guy. Her dad had hired a man partly because he couldn't bear to see another woman sitting at that desk.

Jess had taken the one reserved for a summer intern while they hunted down a fourth desk that would be a decent match for the others. Her dad couldn't wait to bring in the next intern, who'd get the added benefit of her TV news experience. He was so proud of her.

Why, oh why had this had to happen? The calm acceptance she'd managed to find somewhere along the road from Rowdy Ranch into town began to fade. She dragged in another breath.

"It's a wrap!" Her dad flicked off the light in his office and came out beaming. "Did I tell you I got pictures? I was coming back from lunch when Jimmy Holcomb, earbuds blasting, I'm sure, stepped in front of a delivery truck. His dog Shep grabbed him by the seat of his jeans and dragged him back. That truck never could have stopped."

"You got a picture of Shep doing that?"

"Oh, hell, no. I was running and yelling like everyone else. But I got a great shot of Jimmy hugging that big ol' dog and you could see the rip in the back of his jeans, too." He pulled his phone out of his pocket and scrolled through the pictures. "Here you go."

"Excellent!" She enlarged the image. "Jimmy's sure gotten big. He was a pistol when he was two, so I can imagine him bopping around town with earbuds, oblivious. I hope he learned something." She handed back the phone.

"He was pretty shook up, so maybe he did." He tucked the phone away. "Ready to strap on the feed bag?"

"I am, but before we leave…" Her chest felt like Jimmy Holcomb was sitting on it. "I have something to tell you."

Her dad's blue gaze sharpened. "What's wrong?"

"Nothing's wrong, exactly. But something's changed."

"I know."

"You know?"

"Not the *what*, but you've been distracted lately. I figured you'd tell me when you were ready."

The kindness in his voice nearly undid her. She gulped. "I'm pregnant."

He let out a deep sigh. "Thank God."

"Thank God?"

"Monica spotted your car parked in front of Doc Bradley's during your lunch hour on Friday. You know my biggest fear is—"

"I don't have cancer, Dad. I'm a very healthy pregnant lady."

"Beau's?"

"Dad! I've only been in town since August. Who else's would it be?"

He smiled. "Didn't mean to insult you. I also don't want to be an old fuddy-duddy. Times have changed."

"Not that much. Especially in Wagon Train. And before you ask, we used birth control. It... um... failed."

"It happens. Have you told him?"

"An hour ago. That's why I asked to leave early today. I thought he deserved to be the first."

"Quite right. How'd he take it?"

"Like he takes everything. At first he was shocked, but before long he was back to making jokes. Same old Beau."

"It's his defense mechanism, Jess."

"And it's a lousy one. Not everything in life is funny."

"No, but..." He paused. Placing his hands on her shoulders, he held her gaze. "You're not overjoyed about a baby you've accidentally conceived with a man who disappointed you. I get that. But I hope you can eventually be excited about it."

She soaked up his compassion, needing every drop of it. "I promise I will. He or she didn't ask to be born. That's on Beau and me. I intend to give this kid tons of love."

"So will I. Just think. I'll be a granddad."

"You'll be a great one."

He grinned. "You know it, sweetie. C'mon, let's go eat."

And that was that. No drama. Losing his beloved wife had taught her dad to roll with the punches, to look for the gift in the pile of horse poop. She still had a lot of lessons to learn from Andy Hartmann. Acceptance was a big one. Clearly she hadn't mastered it.

3

Beau took Sky up on his offer of a ride over to their mom's house. But first they fed the pigs and settled them into their heated shed for the night.

"That does it." Beau ushered his brother out the mesh gate and latched it behind them. "Thanks for pitching in."

"I get a kick out of those pigs."

"Me, too." He turned up the collar of his sheepskin coat for the walk around to the front of the cabin. Venus, his wishing star when he was a kid, sparkled in the dark navy sky. What would he wish for, now?

"I'm glad you didn't keep the whole lot of them, though."

"Wanted to." His breath fogged the air.

"That would have been a load. You did the right thing, adopting 'em out."

"Probably. But for a few days, I had a herd of pigs. I was a pigboy. That was fun."

"It was chaos. Chopping veggies night and day, building their pen, tending their various ailments, rescheduling your horse training clients. It's a wonder those folks stuck with you."

"No, it's not. I'm the best."

Sky snorted.

"And if I'd kept all those pigs, I wouldn't have had time to get involved with Jess." He opened the passenger door of Sky's silver F-250, climbed in and closed the door.

Sky swung into the driver's seat and pulled his door shut. "You regret that?"

Did he? Sleigh rides, snowball fights, debating where to put her Christmas tree, rolling around in her cozy bed or his big one.... "I don't regret it."

"Right answer." Sky started the truck and the headlights flicked on.

"Why?"

"Because if you regretted getting involved with her, then you might resent the baby. No kid deserves to begin life as the target of resentment."

"You sound like Mom."

"Which means you'll probably hear that from her, too."

"I'm sure." Instead of bothering with his seat belt, he held onto the door handle as Sky navigated around ruts now frozen in place. The road would stay bumpy until spring. "I wonder if Mom felt this disoriented when she found out she was pregnant with you."

"She claims she was happy, even when she knew it wouldn't work out with my dad."

"I hope eventually Jess is happy about our baby. She sure isn't, now."

"Not every woman is as excited about having babies as Mom."

"I doubt *any* woman is."

Sky chuckled. "True."

"Have you ever wondered why none of our dads ever caused problems?"

"Sure did, and finally I asked her. I take it you never did?"

"No." His dad hadn't been around to cause problems. While some of them visited now and then, his never had. Instead he sent a birthday gift every year, expensive souvenirs from various places in the world. "What did she say?"

"She's been lucky that none of them had broken their promise to grant her sole custody. And in return, she didn't ask them to provide any financial—oh hell, bro." He braked the truck. "We can't just pop in to see her."

"No, we sure can't." Beau pulled out his phone and sent her a text. "On Friday I asked how the book was going. She made a face and said she hoped the weekend break would help, but if not, she'd be burning the midnight oil this week."

"She told me the same thing. Can't believe I forgot."

Beau's phone pinged. "She's finished for the day." He sighed. "I was almost hoping—"

"Hey. Not the mood we're going for. Put on your *I can't wait to tell you* face." Sky took his foot off the brake and stepped on the gas pedal.

"Right." Could he fake it? With the woman who knew him the best? Not likely. "Think she'll be upset that I didn't check the condom wrapper for teeth marks?"

"Are you kidding? She'll find it hilarious. She'll want to use it in a book."

"Oh, God."

"She won't if you ask her not to. Hey, I just thought of something. This pregnancy makes Jess a member of the family, right?"

"It does." What a concept.

"Which probably means she needs to know the family secret."

Beau stared at him. "You think?"

"It'll be tough to keep her from finding out if she's around a lot. I'm guessing Mom will want to tell her that the baby's grandma is a bestselling author. Simplifies things for all of us."

"Except Jess."

"On the other hand, she might think it's cool to be in the know."

"You're determined to be positive about this, aren't you?"

"Yes, bro. Yes, I am." Sky turned down the lane leading to the house where he and his siblings had grown up. It had started life as a sad-faced, down-at-the heels bungalow.

At least that was how his mom had described the place. But it sat on a hundred and sixty acres with a spectacular view of the Sapphire Mountains. Pictures from thirty years ago proved the house used to be modest. Not anymore.

As advances and royalty checks had rolled in and more children were born, his mom had added a large bedroom wing for the kids. She'd splurged on a bookcase-lined library and a spacious office, both located on the far side of the house from the kids' rooms.

A kitchen remodeled with vintage appliances featured a window pass-through to the long front porch, a favorite spot for sunset watching on summer evenings. Her Christmas present to the family this year had been a game room with a mirrored bar salvaged from an old saloon.

Slowly she'd created the ranch house of her dreams, including a row of rockers on the porch, a massive stone fireplace in the expanded living/dining room, and furniture right out of *Bonanza.* Beau and his nine siblings had grown up with the smell of sawdust, the whine of saws and the tapping of hammers. The construction noise had drowned out the constant clicking of computer keys as his mom worked to pay for it.

Nowadays, she maintained a less rigorous schedule and only took on a renovation project after she'd turned in a book. With a March first deadline for her fifty-first Western looming, she'd restricted herself from watching home improvement shows on TV and stayed away from Miller's Hardware altogether.

Her truck, an F-350 with a custom purple paint job and a Bigfoot sticker family on the rear window, was the only vehicle in the generous parking area next to the house. Sky was right. His mom loved a good laugh and she'd think the cat story was a riot.

The weight crushing his chest lifted. She'd be tickled by the cat story and she'd cherish her first grandchild. She was nuts about kids. He wasn't bringing her a problem. He was bringing her an unexpected gift.

Sky parked the truck and turned off the motor. "Ready?"

"You know what? I am." He hopped out of the truck and almost beat his brother to the porch.

Sky laughed as he caught up with him. "Don't be leaving your backup in the dust."

"Sorry. I just realized she'll be fine with this."

"Of course she will."

A bark of welcome penetrated the heavy wooden door.

Beau gestured toward the door. "Even Sam will be happy."

"We'll all be happy, bro. It's not like we're the most conventional family in the world. So what if you and Jess aren't a couple? We're used to that dynamic."

"Good point."

His mom opened the door as he reached for the handle. Her copper curls were in disarray, as they usually were when she was deep in a book. She wore her favorite writing outfit, emerald green lounge pants and shirt. "Lucky me!" She stepped back. "Two handsome cowboys have come to call."

"Hey, Mom." He hugged her first and then crouched down to give Sam a thorough head rub and neck scratch.

Sam was a Lassie look-alike, but that wasn't why his mother had picked him out of the selection of shelter dogs. She'd chosen him because he also looked like Sam, John Wayne's sidekick in *Hondo*. Sam and Lassie had been played by the same dog, but not many knew that.

"I'm so glad you two came by." She beamed at them, clearly in a good mood. "You can help me celebrate a stellar writing day."

"Congrats." Sky hung up his coat and hat.

Beau followed suit. "How's the book going now? Any better?"

"I'm won't tempt Fate by saying yes, but the story's coming together."

"Glad to hear it." Beau exchanged an amused glance with Sky. How many times had they heard those words? By next week she could be back in panic mode. He was grateful she wasn't in panic mode tonight.

"C'mon, boys, let's belly up to the bar." She laughed. "I love saying that." She and Sam led the way to the game room. "We need a name for this bar."

"You're the queen of naming things," Sky said.

"But I do that all day. Time for one of you to ante up."

"Rowdy Roost." Beau couldn't say where that had come from. Probably a twist on the hideout in *Butch Cassidy and the Sundance Kid*.

Sky gave him an approving glance. "Not bad, little brother."

"I have my moments."

"I love it, Beau. I'll get a sign made next week." She walked into the dimly lit game room and slipped behind the bar. "What'll you have, gents?"

"Whiskey, please, ma'am." Beau claimed a stool and leaned his elbows on the polished bar. "And leave the bottle."

Her eyebrows shot up. "You have news."

"Yes, ma'am."

"Am I going to like it?"

"I hope so."

She glanced at Sky. "Whiskey for you, too?"

"Might as well."

She lined up three shot glasses, splashed amber liquid into each of them and picked up one. "What are we drinking to?"

Beau held her gaze as he reached for his glass. "Your first grandchild."

Her eyes widened.

"Jess is pregnant."

"I'll be damned."

"But she's very unhappy with him," Sky said, "so I think we should call a family meeting to brainstorm the best strategy for—"

"Ixnay." She shook her head. "We'll meet and brainstorm tomorrow night."

"Why not now?" Sky frowned. "Seems to me the sooner the better."

"Tomorrow night is soon enough. Beau clearly wants to get plastered and I'm of a mind to join him."

"Ah." He put a wealth of understanding in that single syllable.

"You're invited to get drunk with us, of course, and Penny can help us tie one on when she gets home."

"I'll text her to come on over here instead of heading to our place." He pulled out his phone.

"Excellent." Putting down her untouched glass, she leaned toward Beau. "I've been where you are, son." She smiled. "You probably feel like somebody dragged you through a knothole backwards."

"Pretty much."

"I promise this is the best thing that's ever happened to you, including the night you lost your virginity to Sally McGregor."

"You knew about that?"

She just smiled.

Sky put away his phone. "Penny should be here in about thirty minutes."

"Then we'll go slow until then, grab some snacks to soak up the booze." She hoisted her glass. "To your child, Beau, who will be amazing. Welcome to parenthood. You're gonna love it."

4

Jess poked her head into her dad's office. "Monica's back from lunch, so I'm gonna go grab a sandwich."

He pushed his glasses to the top of his head. "Are you planning to stop by the Baby Barn while you're out?"

"Yes, I am."

He smiled. "Attagirl."

"See you." She walked back through the office. Joe's desk was vacant. As usual, he was out schmoozing advertising accounts.

Monica had dived right back into work. Despite wearing a knit cap like Jess's whenever she went outside, she never had hat hair. Her classic gray bob always looked salon perfect.

Purple reading glasses perched on her nose, she scrolled through the breaking news looking for gems that would age well. A weekly couldn't pretend to be the first word on anything, but Wagon Train residents liked getting a glimpse of trends and the story behind the story.

Jess stopped by Monica's desk. "I'll be back by one-thirty."

She glanced over the rim of her glasses. "No rush. Looks like a slow news day." Her usually sharp gaze softened. "Good luck at the Baby Barn."

"Would you believe I've never been inside the place?"

"Why would you? I've only gone when I was invited to a baby shower. Prepare yourself. It's so sweet you'll need an insulin shot when you get back."

"Dad warned me. Who buys little cowboy vests and boots for a newborn? How crazy is that?"

"Don't laugh. I've bought those very things for a baby shower and they were the hit of the party."

"But a newborn doesn't need—"

"Evidently the parents of the newborn do."

"Not this parent. I promise to come back with sensible stuff."

Monica smiled. "Can't wait to see how this turns out."

"Don't worry. I'm not into wasting money." She pulled on her hat, buttoned her coat and headed out the door.

After a three-minute walk down Main Street, she stood in front of the Baby Barn. Stacked hay bales served as display shelves in the front window. The entrance was a scaled-down barn door. Nothing overly sweet about any of that.

But an explosion of heart-themed merchandise nearly obscured the no-nonsense hay bales. Every plush animal held a heart pillow or wore a bow decorated in hearts. February. The month where Valentine's Day lived. Don't care, don't care, don't care.

The Baby Barn did, though. Embroidered hearts decorated nearly every item of clothing — tiny fringed vests, plaid yoked shirts, denim pull-on pants, small cowboy hats, chaps... chaps? For a baby? With embroidered hearts, no less? Sheesh.

A set of blocks spelled *I LOVE YOU.* Candy hearts filled a miniature buckboard. Two ragdolls, one dressed as a cowgirl and one in a cowboy outfit, sat on the buckboard, arms entwined.

Maybe she wouldn't shop today. She had gobs of time. March was soon enough to start, even April. Or she could wait for the Memorial Day sales. If she bought clothes and toys before the tourists arrived in June, she'd be fine.

Except over dinner with her dad, she'd promised to buy something for the baby today as a symbolic gesture. They'd agreed that shopping for the little guy or gal was a good first step in acceptance. It might even spark a little happiness, connect some positivity to the blessed event.

She took a deep breath, slid open the faux barn door and walked in. A sound system played Tim McGraw's *My Little Girl.* Her dad's favorite. The song made her teary under normal circumstances.

Better get out of here before I lose it. Clearing her tight throat, she headed back toward the door.

"Jessica? Jessica Hartmann? Is that you?"

She swiped at her eyes and turned around. "Yes." A sweet-faced woman walked toward her. "Miss Gentry?"

"It's Mrs. Harrison, honey."

"I knew that." She flushed. "It was on the society page of the *Sentinel* when I was in sixth grade. But I guess you'll always be Miss Gentry in my head."

"I still answer to it. I love hearing someone address me by that name. Then I know it's one of my first-graders from the early days." She smiled. "Think you could call me Denise?"

"Never."

Her smile broadened. "That's what everyone says. You're like a bunch of puppies who were trained to stay behind a gate you could easily jump as adults."

"Exactly." Jess returned her smile. "Since you're not wearing a coat, either you work here or—"

"I own the place."

"Really? You're not teaching anymore?"

"Nope." She quickly scanned the store. "Good, my browsers are still browsing." She turned back to Jess. "I opened the Baby Barn three years ago. I loved teaching but I've always dreamed of owning a shop like this."

"I'll be darned."

"It's been great. But I should let you go wherever you're off to. I just couldn't stop myself from at least saying hello before you left."

That was her cue. She could take the coward's way out and pretend she had urgent business elsewhere. "I thought I needed to go, but turns out I don't, after all."

"Then what can I help you find?"

"A special gift for a newborn."

"Wonderful! Who's the lucky mom?"

"Me."

Her eyes widened, but she recovered fast. An elementary teacher skill, no doubt. "That's fabulous. How soon?"

"August."

"So you're just beginning! How exciting for you."

"It is, but the baby's father and I, we're... we're not..."

"Say no more, honey." She patted Jess's arm. "Do you want to look at outfits or toys?"

"Toys. Make that bears."

"Right this way." She headed toward the right wall. "Bears are so classic. These days you can buy a plush animal of almost any creature imaginable, but I love teddy bears the most."

"I still have mine. His name's Wally."

"Cute name. I made the mistake of giving mine away when I got married — probably another reason I wanted to open this shop. I'm surrounded by teddy bears. Here you go." She gestured toward shelves of plush animals, everything from anteaters to zebras.

But the bear population outnumbered them all. Jess gravitated to that section.

"I'll leave you to it." She touched Jess's arm. "Looks like one of the browsers has made it to the cash register."

"You're here alone?"

"Not normally. Adele's on her lunch break."

"Then by all means take care of business."

"I'll check back in a few minutes."

"No rush." Jess studied each bear, her hand over her stomach. Would this baby want a sturdy guy like Wally? His brown fur was rubbed off in places from constant contact with her grasping fingers and gnawing baby teeth.

Or would her child need a softer, more padded version to hug and snuggle with? "What do you think, little one?" Yikes. She'd started talking to the kid. Spooky.

"*I want the one with movable arms and legs, please, Mommy.*" The high-pitched voice came from somewhere behind her.

She turned around. A grey sock puppet with mouse ears and googly eyes stared back at her. The puppeteer was mostly hidden behind the shelving, but the black crown of a Stetson and the faint scent of a familiar shaving lotion sent her heart into overdrive.

What Beau was doing here was anybody's guess. Maybe his mom had given him the same advice — take the first step and buy something for the baby. "Why movable arms and legs?"

"*Because they're cooool!*" The puppet's mouth opened wide.

She laughed. Couldn't help it. "They're also the most expensive bears on the shelf."

"I could get you some extra moola."

"Oh, could you, now?"

"There's this guy I know, he's a soft touch."

"I know that guy. He's also soft in the head."

"Ooooo, nice burn!"

"Thank you."

"Wanna meet this softie?"

"Already did, thanks."

"You just think you have. You ain't seen nuthin, yet. Beau McLintock, come on down! Or up. Come on up here and say hello to the nice lady."

"I dunno, Mousy." Beau switched to the velvet baritone that made the ladies swoon. "She doesn't sound eager."

"Aw, c'mon. Don't be a scaredy cat. And speaking of cats, have you heard the one about—"

"Beau. Stop it."

He straightened, his six-foot-three frame rising over the shelving, his chocolate gaze meeting hers.

She'd been a sucker for those big brown eyes ever since... sheesh, fourth grade. They still made her stomach go wonky. "Fancy meeting you here."

"Stole my line."

"I promised my dad I'd come in and buy a token gift for..."

"Maverick."

"What?"

"It's a good name. Might even be gender neutral these days. I—"

"You're already dreaming up names?"

"You're not?"

"I've known about this for less than three days. I don't really believe it yet."

He gave a slow nod. "Mom figured we'd come at it from different angles."

"How so?"

"When I was growing up, Mom would announce she was pregnant again and we'd start tossing around names that very day."

Clearly because they were excited about the new arrival. Rowdy Ranch was a happy place, steered in that direction by the positive influence of its owner. Jess liked Desiree McLintock. Liked the entire family, in fact. That had made the breakup even more difficult. "How did she take the news?"

"Better than I did. She's confident we'll find a workable compromise."

"And the rest of your family?"

"Sky and Penny are the only ones besides Mom who know. The rest will find out tonight at a family meeting."

"Oh."

"That's why I drove in today. I stopped by the *Sentinel* to ask if you'd come to the meeting. And stay for dinner."

Her breath caught. "Whose idea was that?"

"Mom's, but I'm on board with it. If we present a united front, they'll be reassured that we can handle this without drama."

"Can we?"

"Hey, I'm not the one who shook up the bottle of champagne and sprayed it on yours truly."

"I'm not proud of that. Maybe I should have guessed you'd think of marriage as a joke, but I... didn't."

Regret flashed in his eyes. Then he glanced away. "Bad timing on my part."

"Is that how you see it?"

"Absolutely." He cleared his throat and a familiar gleam of mischief lit his gaze. "I learned something that night."

"What?"

"Never joke about marriage when a woman's holding an uncorked bottle of champagne."

She stared at him.

"I'm kidding. I shouldn't have said what I did."

"On the contrary. It was a blessing in disguise. I discovered how you really feel about the subject."

"I wouldn't say that. It's a complicated concept and I—"

"Never mind." A complicated concept that made him so uncomfortable he had to make fun of it. "I'll come to the family meeting. What time?"

"I'll pick you up at five-thirty, if that's okay."

"Thanks, but I'll drive myself. Should I be there around six?"

"Let me fetch you. We're supposed to get snow and my truck's better equipped to deal with—"

"I'll be fine."

"You'll be safer if I drive you there and back. That way you won't be alone on the road."

She looked away. "Which is what I'd prefer, instead of spending all that time in your—"

"I know." He sucked in a breath. "Hell, I can't believe I'm saying this, but... please do it for the baby."

Startled, she glanced back at him. "Oh." The implications of that request stretched far into the future. Until now, she hadn't fully grasped how much her life had changed. He had a right to ask this of her. "I'll be ready at five-thirty."

5

Beau pulled up in front of the bungalow Jess called home, a place she'd found for rent that was only a block away from her dad's house. That put her close enough to share the occasional dinner with him. What did Andy Hartmann think about this turn of events?

When Beau had stopped by the *Sentinel* today, Andy had been back in his office on the phone. He'd raised a hand in greeting and Beau had tipped his hat. Tracking down Jess had been a top priority, so he'd left after getting the word from Monica.

A talk with Jess's father was on his to-do list, likely tomorrow, not that he looked forward to the conversation. But it was the thing to do.

He was halfway up the walk to Jess's front porch when she came out, closing the door while pulling on her coat. The message was clear — she didn't want him inside her house.

She'd tamed her glorious dark-red hair with a clip at her nape and pulled on a knit hat. When he'd walked into the Baby Barn he'd zeroed in on the bright waves falling freely to her shoulders. God, he loved her hair.

And her mouth, and her eyes and her....

"No snow yet." She said it with a saucy tilt to her head, as if pointing out that he was chauffeuring her for no reason.

"It'll come. I can smell it." He turned and kept pace with her on the way back to the truck. He'd never expected her to ride in it again.

"Beau McLintock, super nose."

"It's a valuable skill." As he opened the passenger door, the light floral scent of her perfume teased his libido. She didn't use much, but she liked dabbing it in all her secret places. When she was aroused — nope, forbidden topic.

She let him help her into the truck. Maybe from habit. Whatever her motivation, he'd take it. She hadn't bothered with gloves and neither had he. The skin-to-skin contact gave him a jolt of adrenaline that lasted until he'd rounded the truck and climbed into the driver's seat.

He closed the door, buckled up and started the engine. "Did you get the bear with the movable arms and legs?" He put the truck in gear and pulled away from the curb.

"Yes, but only because Miss Gentry, I mean, Mrs. Harrison, said being able to manipulate the arms and legs was a good developmental tool."

"Exactly. He can walk around, shake hands, kick a ball, signal a—"

"*She.*"

"Excuse me?"

"*She* can walk around and shake hands. The bear's a girl."

"How can you tell?"

"She has a sweet face."

"It's been said that I have a sweet face."

"By whom?"

"My mother."

"Maybe when you were two, but you don't have a sweet face anymore."

"What would you call it, then?"

Captivating. Irresistible. Seductive. "The face of a rogue."

"You wound me, dear lady."

"I tell it like it is."

"I don't suppose you'd let me buy a half-interest in that bear."

"You suppose right."

"That's okay. When Maverick's old enough, I'll tell him or her I was a consultant on the bear purchase. He or she will want to know that."

"We're not naming this child Maverick."

"I looked it up today. It means *independent* and it's definitely unisex. And getting more popular by the—"

"I don't want to chase trends."

"My mom likes it."

"Not surprising, considering how much she loves Western names."

"We all favor them. Last night Mom, me, Sky and Penny sat around dreaming up names. It was like old times, except it's even more fun when you're sipping good whiskey."

Jess took a deep breath. "I'm a big fan of tradition, but you guys don't get to decide the baby's name. Not all by yourselves, anyway."

"Okay. I just wanted to throw it out there because it seems exactly right. Maybe it'll grow on you."

"I don't think so."

"You never know. We named Mom's bar last night, too. Rowdy Roost. We considered a few other names for the baby, but Maverick was the favorite."

"I'm amazed it wasn't used for one of you."

"Bret was almost named Maverick, but Sky lobbied for something with less syllables, so it'd be easier for us younger kids to say."

"That sounds like Sky." She hesitated. "Why isn't he named for a Western TV or movie character?"

"She wasn't into that yet." He'd learned to give that answer years ago.

"I was convinced there was a fascinating story behind those names. That's why I wanted to do a feature on her and your family last fall."

"And here I thought you'd pitched the idea to get my attention."

"Aren't you exhausted carrying around your big ol' ego?"

"Nah, I'm used to it."

"Sorry to burst your bubble, but you weren't my motivation. It was pure coincidence that you happened to be around when I drove out to talk with her."

"It wasn't a coincidence."

"You came up to the house on purpose to see me?"

"Yes, ma'am." His mom had asked him to sit in on the interview. His talent for creating welcome distractions would have come in handy if Jess had accidentally pulled on a loose thread in the carefully woven tale of Desiree McLintock.

"What if I hadn't set up that interview? Would you have made another opportunity to ask me out?"

"Probably." A few brief sightings since her return had piqued his interest.

"Then we would have ended up dating anyway. I wasn't the instigator."

"Does it matter?"

She glanced at him. "I guess not. But the baby has me playing the *what if* game, especially since my reporter's instincts steered me wrong on the naming thing. I didn't have a story, after all."

"Mm." Her instincts had been right on target. She'd learn the truth tonight and she still wouldn't be able to write about it.

"I like your mom. She and that book club she has, Wenches Who Read, were so kind when my mom passed."

"Your mom was a valuable member of the group." And that fine lady had kept the secret. He had confidence that her daughter would, too.

"I was afraid breaking up with you would mean I couldn't be friends with Miss Desiree anymore. I mean, *Desiree.* She begged me to drop the *Miss* I learned to use when I was a kid. I had visions of us getting to know each other even better, but now…."

"You're carrying her first grandchild. She'll want to be friends."

"I'm glad." She paused. "You know, I'm just now beginning to absorb the ramifications of this."

"You and me, both."

"We've made your mom and my dad grandparents."

"Yes, ma'am. And my brothers will be uncles. My sister will be Aunt Angelique. Or Aunt Angie. She's going by that more often, now."

"Then there's Buck and Marybeth. I'm not clear how they're related to you. Aunt and Uncle?"

"The Weavers aren't related at all. Mom hired them to help her with the ranch work and raising us. That was—wow—twenty-nine years ago. We feel related to them, though. They're like adopted grandparents."

"Will they be at the family meeting?"

"I'm sure. This is a big deal."

"I know." She sighed. "I wish it wasn't so... unplanned."

"Me, too."

"It's out of order. Your family is great and I'm sure they'll roll with it, but this should be a Sky and Penny announcement."

"If you're trying to create a timetable that makes sense, it's not Sky and Penny. They didn't get together until right before Christmas."

"So we got the jump on them."

He smiled. "How you talk."

"I didn't mean it like that."

"I know you didn't, but I like the way you said it, like we won a race. To be honest, I'm secretly tickled that Mom's first grandchild will be my kid and not Sky's. He's always first in everything."

Jess chuckled.

The sound cheered him. He liked making her laugh. Which was his downfall, apparently. "Well, he is."

"Sibling rivalry. Something I know nothing about. I never had to share my folks with a brother or sister."

"Speaking of that, your dad gave me a wave when I walked into the *Sentinel* office today. Does that mean he doesn't want to cut out my heart with a rusty knife?'

"He does not. I told him it was Midnight's fault."

"Thanks, but much as I long to blame this on your cat, I can't. I dropped the condoms on the floor. I knew you had a cat. I know cats like to chew on whatever they find, especially if it crinkles. I should have inspected those condoms before using them."

"That's assuming your brain was in gear."

"No excuse. My cock was a loaded gun. A functional condom is the safety. It's my job to make sure the safety is engaged before I handle the gun."

"I think I was the one handling it."

He choked out a laugh. And his jeans began to pinch. "Do you really want to go there?"

Her voice was tight. "Nope, sure don't. Sorry. My bad."

Silence descended. Sort of. Her breathing wasn't exactly regular. His wasn't, either.

She cleared her throat. "Animal magnetism is what got us into this situation. I'm not going to allow that to—"

"Yeah, me, either." He took a steadying breath. "Although we wouldn't have to worry that you'd get pregnant again."

A raspy noise in the back of her throat could be swallowed laughter. Or the sound of extreme exasperation. He'd go with laughter. It *was* funny, damn it.

6

Jess sighed. The Beau McLintock effect. Ten minutes alone with him and she was making salacious remarks. He could get her out of her clothes faster than any man she'd known. He could short-circuit her inhibitions even faster than that.

Maybe she hadn't started this thing, but she'd moved it along by accepting a date when he'd walked her back to the car on that fateful afternoon. She'd deliberately embarked on a fling with the cowboy who'd tempted her for years. She'd ignored the time-worn advice that no birth control method is foolproof.

Lured by the feel-good vibes of Christmas and wonderful sex, she'd told herself she and Beau had something special. She wasn't just another girlfriend who'd be dropped in a few weeks. The reasons for her self-delusion didn't matter.

The consequences did. Her neck and shoulder muscles tensed when Beau rounded a turn and lights from the ranch house pierced the darkness. She'd been here three times, once for the interview and twice in December — for the Yule party on the twenty-first and again on Christmas Eve.

The house had dazzled her each time. Perched on a slight rise that provided breathtaking views, the rambling structure sparkled with fairy lights along the eaves and wrapped around the porch posts. For Christmas they'd been multicolored. Tonight they were a warm white. More strands wound through the branches of several leafless oaks, adding to the magical aura.

Desiree had planted the trees as saplings and placed them strategically so they wouldn't block her sight lines. She'd told Jess she wanted a glimpse of the mountains from as many windows as possible. Their majesty inspired her, and fairy lights balanced their masculinity — yin and yang.

Beau's beautiful and classy mom intrigued her. Intimidated her a little, too. Although she hadn't spent much time with Desiree, her mother had. Her mom had cherished her membership in the Wenches Who Read. Upon her death five years ago, the WWR had made a sizeable donation to the Wagon Train Public Library in her name.

Local gossip hinted that Desiree had come from money. Her bookstore in town couldn't possibly earn enough to finance this ranch and a brood of ten. Beau had said everyone was self-supporting now, but ten kids would have been a financial drain in the early years.

Ford trucks and only Ford trucks sat in the parking area. Another tradition. Beau pulled in beside a black one. "Cheyenne must have found someone to take his shift at the fire station."

"Has he let his hair grow out at all?" In high school she hadn't been able to tell him apart from his twin Clint, but these days Clint favored collar-length hair and Cheyenne wore a buzz cut.

"No, ma'am. In fact, he's threatened to shave his head to simplify his life."

"Did you say he got off work to be here?"

"Mom put out a Code Red. You don't ignore a Code Red."

"They were all *summoned*?"

"Not like you're thinking. If anyone has a major conflict, they'll be excused. Otherwise, we're obligated to respond to a Code Red. It's not because Mom's a tyrant. It's out of respect for each other." He parked the truck and unsnapped his seat belt. "The parking lot's slushy. Let me help you—"

"Wait." She gripped his arm. Solid muscle flexed under his sheepskin jacket. Not so long ago she'd reveled in his deliciously fit body. No more. *No more.* Despite the tingling in her lady parts.

"What?" He sounded impatient.

"We haven't discussed how we're going to do this. What the setup will be. Your mom wants us to present a united front, but what does that mean, exactly?"

"Regarding setup, a family meeting is traditionally held in the living room. In the winter, Mom builds a fire. We get ourselves drinks and there's always munchies on the coffee table. Ready to go in?"

"Almost. Wish I could have a stiff drink to get through this."

"Stage fright?" His tone was softer, less businesslike.

"A little."

"They like you. They'll be nice."

"I know, but…"

"Tell you what." His voice gentled even more. "I won't drink alcohol tonight, either. For solidarity."

She glanced at him. "That's very thoughtful. Thank you."

"You're welcome." He turned in her direction and gave her the trademark Beau McLintock smile. "Anything else?"

"Yes." She wanted to be immune from that smile, unaffected by the heat simmering in his eyes. Instead, her skin flushed and she struggled to take in air. *Concentrate.* "Do you want to do it?" Damn it, she sounded like a breathless teenager.

His smile morphed into a sexy grin. "Anytime you want, sweet lady."

Whoops. Miscommunication. Heart hammering, she fought the urge to grab him. "I was…" She gulped. "I was talking about who would make the announcement to your family."

His tone turned brisk. "I knew that's what you meant."

"No, you didn't. Your pupils dilated."

"You can't tell in this light."

"I can so." She took a shaky breath. "I can see your face in the glow from that tree."

"My *sweet* face?" He'd shifted back to seductive mode, murmuring the words and leaning toward her, bringing with him the scent of pine and aroused male.

"Don't you dare kiss me."

His voice lowered another notch. "You want me to."

"No, I don't." *Liar.*

"I have evidence. You're breathing fast. And you're holding onto my coat."

"*Ahhh!*" She let go of the supple suede and flung herself toward the passenger door. "How do you do that?"

He straightened and draped one hand over the steering wheel, a casual gesture at odds with the rapid rise and fall of his chest. "Do what?"

"Make me forget everything else."

He gazed at her, his fingers tightening on the wheel. "You affect me the same way, Jess."

"Hard to believe."

"I insisted on giving you a ride out here because thinking of you driving through a storm made me crazy. I promised myself I'd handle the intimacy of my truck's cab without cracking."

"Riding out here together was a bad idea."

"It was a good idea that required a fast exit from the cozy truck. But you wanted to chat when I have nothing to do with my hands."

She gulped. "Sorry."

"Two minutes ago I was seriously considering grabbing a quickie. Even though my family is waiting." Intensity rippled in his voice. "How deranged is that?"

Her loud heartbeat made her ears buzz. "I... I was thinking of it, too."

"You would have hated yourself. And me."

"Mostly myself."

"Let's get out of here." Turning away, he opened the driver's door, letting in an icy blast of cold air. "Before we do something we'll both regret."

"Good plan." She unfastened her belt and opened her door.

"Hang on. Like I said, it's slushy."

"Don't forget I was born here, too." She climbed down and placed a tentative boot on the ground. Yep, like stepping into a frozen margarita. She'd choose that over a sheet of solid ice, though.

He made it around the back of the truck and held out his hand.

"Thanks, but I don't need—"

"Helping a woman over dicey terrain is what cowboys do. Anyone who was born here would know that."

"You win." Holding his gaze, she placed her hand in his.

He maintained eye contact as he threaded his fingers through hers and tightened his grip. "We were good together, Jess."

Her heart lurched. Her physical connection with Beau had transcended time and space. But amazing sex wasn't enough. She wanted someone who believed in forever.

7

It wasn't over. Whatever Beau had created with Jess —and he wasn't talking about the baby— still existed. He saw it in her eyes. But after his jokes about marriage on Christmas Eve, she didn't trust him.

No surprise there. He didn't trust himself. What did he know about happily ever after? None of the McLintocks knew, not even his mother. Sky had closed his eyes and jumped into matrimony. Beau didn't have that kind of faith.

But as he walked toward his mother's house hand-in-hand with Jess, pride swelled in his chest. She was carrying their baby. Without that connection, he'd be yesterday's news. Now she couldn't easily dismiss him. That gave him room to maneuver. To figure out a few things.

A snowflake drifted down, followed by another, and another. "Snow's coming."

"I noticed." Her warm breath fogged the air. "You never said which one of us should make the announcement."

"I should probably make it and then turn the mic over to you."

"We'll have a mic?"

"A metaphorical mic. Didn't mean to scare you."

"Too late."

"Hey, didn't you anchor the six o'clock news in the big city?"

"If you're implying my on-camera experience gives me an edge, you'd be dead wrong. I stared into a lens and delivered news to a faceless audience."

"You could pretend you were doing that."

"I'm sure your family would *love* that kind of delivery."

"How about holding my hand while we tell them?"

"That actually might help me."

"I wasn't thinking of you. I need to hold someone's hand and grabbing Sky's would be weird."

"Come on, you're not afraid."

"That's what you think. I'm shaking in my boots."

"You? The fearless Beau McLintock?"

"I'm not as together as I look." The snow fell faster as they mounted the steps and crossed the porch to the massive front door. "This is damned scary."

"It's your family. They love you."

He paused to wipe his boots on the thick doormat. "You don't understand." His gut clenched. "I'm the one who's always lecturing them about safe sex, the one who makes sure everyone has a generous supply of condoms. I'm the savvy smart mouth who'll never be caught with his pants down. And yet..."

"Listen, blame Midnight." She wiped her feet. "You probably thought I'd shut him out of the room."

"I was oblivious to that cat. Or anything but you. The house could have burned to the ground and I wouldn't have noticed. Or cared." He put his hand on the door handle.

"Don't tell them that. Extreme lust is not a valid excuse."

"It's better than extreme stupidity. But you know what? I'm not making any excuses. This happened. We'll deal with it."

"I like that approa—"

A sharp bark cut her off and the door swung open. His mom had chosen her purple power outfit — slim-fitting pants and a sweater studded with rhinestones. Sam moved up beside her, wagging his plume of a tail. Voices and laughter drifted from the living room at the back of the house.

"Hi, there, kids. Sam heard you. Come on in." She backed away from the door with a hand on Sam's collar.

He ushered Jess inside and closed the door. "It's starting to snow."

"I see that. You have flakes on your hat." She smiled at Jess. "You look freaked out."

"Because I am."

"We all like you very much. You don't have to be afraid of us."

"Thanks, Miss—" She gulped and started over. "Thanks, Desiree, but never in my wildest dreams did I think—"

"Jess." His mom took her by the shoulders. "This baby is great news. *Great.*" She glanced at him. "Let go of her, son. I want to hug the mother of my grandchild."

His heart squeezed with regret. If he hadn't made those bonehead comments on Christmas Eve, this moment could have been joyous instead of bittersweet.

His mom pulled Jess into a tight embrace and murmured a few soft words before she released her and cleared her throat. "I know this was unexpected, but everything happens for a reason."

"My dad said that, too." Jess unbuttoned her coat and started to take it off.

When Beau moved in to help her with it, she didn't shy away. It was a small thing, but it gave him hope. He hung it up and added his jacket and hat to the coat tree in the entry.

"I'd expect a philosophical response from Andy." His mother let out a breath. "I wish your mom—"

"Me, too." Jess said it fast and gulped.

He started to put a comforting arm around her shoulders. And hesitated, unsure if she'd welcome comfort from him.

Sam didn't hesitate. He padded over and pressed his head against her thigh. Giving all her attention to the collie, she thrust her fingers into his luxurious ruff and scratched the top of his head.

Sam had all the luck.

"I'd like to offer myself as a surrogate support system." His mom sounded tentative, not her usual M.O. "Me and the Wenches, if that would be—"

"You've told them?" Jess's head lifted and her eyes grew wide.

"No, I—"

"Geez, Desiree, I'm sorry." Jess winced. "You have every right to tell them. I told Mrs. Harrison today. If I'm blabbing the news to my first-grade teacher, you can certainly inform your best friends."

"I haven't said a word to anyone, and I won't until you and Beau make your announcement tonight. Everybody's here except Lucky and Marsh. Oh, and Buck."

Beau glanced at her. "I take it Marsh had a medical emergency?"

"Afraid so. A client's beloved mare went into early labor. And a pipe sprung a leak at the bookstore, so Lucky's dealing with it. Buck drove into town so he could—"

"A leak?" L'Amour and More was his mother's pride and joy. Damaged books would wound her soul. "Shouldn't you be there, too?"

"I'm right where I want to be. I trust those two. They'd handle it."

"I'm sure they will, but we should get this program rolling. The sooner Jess and I relay our news, the sooner you can go check on things at the store. Although with the storm coming, one of us should go with you, in case—"

"Easy, son." She laid a hand on his arm. "I'm staying for the duration. This is more important than my store."

Those words had come out of her mouth only once before, when nine-year-old Rance had fallen from his horse and given himself a concussion on the store's opening day. His little brother had a talent for poor timing.

"Let's get you two something to drink before you head in." She ushered them through the arched door on her right.

Sam followed her in, ears pricked, tail waving.

"No, Sam, nothing for you."

The wagging slowed.

"Go find Sky." She pointed to the living room. "That's a good boy. Go find Sky and Penny!"

He trotted down the hall, nails clicking on the hardwood floor.

"Why not give him a treat, Mom?"

"I'm scaling back so he doesn't get fat." She gestured toward the counter. "Somebody will likely give him some chips, anyway." Bags of various types of chips lay on the counter, along with cans of mixed nuts and two empty six-pack cartons. "What'll you have to drink, Jess? I know what my son wants."

"Not necessarily. I'll have whatever Jess is having."

His mother's eyebrows lifted.

"If she can't drink booze, I won't, either."

She gave him a nod of approval. "How about some virgin apple cider from last month's visit to the Buckskin?"

"That would be perfect." He turned to Jess. "I think you'll like it."

"Sounds good to me."

His mom took two bottles from the fridge. "Want me to warm it up?"

"Not for me, thanks," Jess said. "Something cool going down my throat would be lovely."

"That's easy, then." She handed him both bottles. "I'll let you take off the caps, son. My wrists are complaining today."

Jess frowned. "How come?"

"Just my tendonitis acting up." She winked at Beau. "A little too much typing, I guess."

"There's an understatement." He twisted off the caps and gave a bottle to Jess.

"Typing?" Jess looked confused. And curious. "Are you and the Wenches into a new project of some kind?"

"I suppose that's one way of putting it. You'll get more information tonight." His mother grabbed an alcoholic cider for herself and held it out for him to open. "You have something to tell the family and the family has something to tell you."

"Oh?" She gave him a questioning glance.

"The McLintock family secret." He returned the open bottle to his mom.

"Does it have anything to do with your last name? I always wondered about—"

"Later, dear girl," his mom said. "It'll be better if we take things in order."

"Yes, ma'am." She sent him another puzzled look.

He flashed her a smile. He'd be glad once she knew the truth. He'd kept the secret while they'd dated, and what a pain. He'd been monitoring his speech all his life and should have been used to it, but leaving Jess in the dark had stuck in his craw.

"Here's to the baby." His mom tapped her bottle against each of theirs. "Let's do this." Turning, she led the way down the hall to the increasingly noisy living room.

When they walked in, Rance let out a whoop and strode over, followed by the rest of the family. "Finally! Welcome back, Jess! I was stoked to hear you'd be here."

"Thanks, Rance."

"Clearly you're the reason for this family meeting." He picked up her left hand. "What? No ring?"

"Rance." Their mother's voice contained a hint of steel. "Mind your manners."

"Sorry, ma'am." He rubbed the back of his neck. "But I was hopin' to see a rock on her finger. She fits into this family way better than any of the women Beau—"

"*Rance.*" She gave him a look that would reduce a lesser man to rubble.

He just smiled and winked at Beau. "I expect the ring's on order."

Beau sighed and shook his head. His irrepressible little brother's style was familiar. Not surprising since Rance had followed him around from the day he could walk, imitating his every move.

The others came over, clearly eager to see Jess again. She'd been popular with his family. The twins remembered her from high school. The others hadn't interacted with her back then, but she'd quickly made friends with them at the Yule party.

Angie had pestered her with questions about her TV career and Marybeth had been eager to hear about celebrity sightings. Christmas Eve had sealed the deal. Jess had been a hit.

The meet and greet threatened to go on forever, especially since Penny had never met Jess, which gave those two plenty to talk about. Sam picked up on the mood and roamed from one friendly scratch to another, accepting any offered chips along the way.

Beau finally made eye contact with Sky.

His big brother gave a quick nod and whistled for silence. "The McLintock family meeting is in session. Please take your seats."

Everyone returned to the spot they'd claimed earlier. Sam curled up in his monogrammed doggie bed by the fire.

Sky gave the crowd a once-over and nodded. "Beau and Jess, you have the floor."

Holding out his hand to Jess, he led her over near the fireplace. His siblings grinned at him, obviously certain an engagement was about to be announced. This sucked.

He took a deep breath. "Jess and I recently learned something that will affect us, but will affect all of you, too."

The grins faded.

"In approximately seven months, we'll be parents."

The collective gasp of surprise was damned embarrassing. He cleared his throat. "I won't lie to you. It was an accident."

"You're kidding." Clint gazed at him in disbelief. His shock was mirrored by the rest of them.

"I'm not kidding. We didn't intend this to happen, but now that it has, we—"

"I'm gonna be Uncle Rance?" His little brother's expression had shifted from dismay to excitement.

"That's right." He surveyed the group. Bret, Gil and the twins clearly didn't share Rance's positive reaction. Their mouths remained set in a grim line.

Rance stood and gestured around the room. "Hey, you guys, we'll all be uncles, except Angie, who'll be an aunt. That's pretty cool."

"Maybe for us," Cheyenne pointed out, "but you don't see Beau and Jess jumping for joy."

"Maybe because they'll end up with all the work." Rance paused. "Unless Mom decides to help. Oh, my God, Mom. You'll be a *grandma*." He stared at her. "You don't look like one, though."

His mom smiled. "Sure I do, son. The stereotypes don't fit anymore."

"Well, *I* certainly fit Rance's image of a grandmother." Diminutive Marybeth sat in one of the leather easy chairs, her feet dangling. She pulled her long braid over her shoulder. "Or maybe I'm more like a great-grandmother. I'll give you and Jess all the help you need with that little one."

"I will, too." Angie's curly dark hair was still damp, clearly from a recent shower. Without makeup and dressed in sweats, she looked much younger than twenty-three. "But I can tell you're not overjoyed about this, big brother."

"I wouldn't say that. I—"

"You're not smiling. You're always smiling. Anyway, could we please hear what Jess has to say about this turn of events?"

"Of course." He turned to her. "You're up." The lack of sparkle in her eyes wasn't encouraging. He held his breath.

She glanced around the room. "You're a wonderful family and I'm honored to be having a baby who will be part of it." A slight tremor ran through her words. "By association, I'll be a part of the family, too, and I look forward to that." She paused to clear her throat.

"We're delighted to have you," his mom said with an encouraging smile.

Jess looked her way. "Thanks, Desiree. That means a lot." She squared her shoulders and faced the group again. "You may be wondering if Beau and I will get back together because of this pregnancy." Her voice was stronger, now. "That isn't going to happen."

He exhaled. She couldn't be more specific than that. In her estimation, their relationship was doomed.

8

Jess's brief speech wasn't a crowd pleaser. Disappointment hung in the air as the siblings exchanged sad glances and shrugs of resignation.

She soldiered on. "That said, we'll co-parent this baby the best way we know how." She turned to Beau. "Right?"

"Absolutely." His jaw was tight. "The welfare of this kid is all that matters."

"Can I say something?" Marybeth scooted to the edge of her chair and hopped down. At five-foot nothing, she looked like an elf as she extricated herself from the generously sized piece of furniture.

Beau snapped to attention. "Yes, ma'am."

"Good. Got something on my mind." She came toward them with a slightly bow-legged stride, stuck her thumbs in the belt loops of her faded jeans and lifted her chin until she was eye-to-eye with Beau. "It appears you have a situation, son."

"Yes, ma'am." Pink tinged his cheeks.

"On Christmas Eve, this young lady seemed to think the world of you. When you two left the party, I was expecting to see her again for

Christmas dinner. I believe we'd invited her father, too."

"We did." His blush deepened.

"Instead she vamoosed. I wasn't going to get into it, figured it was none of my business, but this baby changes things. You must have royally screwed up that night, son."

One of his brothers snickered. Jess couldn't tell which one, but a quick assessment indicted they were all enjoying the heck out of this. A couple had left their seats and wandered closer.

"Yes, ma'am." Beau's gaze lowered and he stared at his boots.

"Maybe you've shared the details with some of the folks here, but I—"

"I haven't. Didn't think it was necessary."

"It wasn't before, but it is, now. Cards on the table, son."

Jess sucked in a breath. Really?

Beau tightened his grip on her hand and lifted his head to look at her, his expression bleak. Then he returned his attention to Marybeth. "After we left the party, Jess let me know that she wouldn't be in town for New Year's because she was flying to Philadelphia for a friend's wedding."

Her initial anger had congealed into sorrow. He'd ruined Christmas Eve and tainted her enjoyment of her friend's wedding.

"I made a lame joke about marriage. When I didn't get the reaction I'd expected, I doubled down and made another joke and... a third one."

Several of his siblings groaned. Those who weren't already standing rose to their feet as everyone formed a semi-circle around the unfolding drama.

Marybeth glowered at him. "Why on earth would you do such a thing?"

"Because I'm an idiot."

"I'd have to agree with you, there. It won't be easy to clean up a mess like that."

Whoa. Time to dive in. Jess swallowed. "Excuse me, Marybeth, but I don't want to clean it up. I'm moving on."

"I totally understand that urge, honey. Maybe that's the best thing to do. But I believe you cared for him once. Otherwise his jokes wouldn't have made you so upset."

Oh, boy. "Could we discuss this later? I could meet you for coffee next week."

One of Beau's brothers chuckled. Another one muttered *nice try.*

"This is how it tends to go with family meetings, Jess," Angie said. "We like to get things out in the open. I think I can speak for everyone that we want to hear your side of it."

"Alrighty, then." She extricated her hand from Beau's tight grip and addressed the group. "I was getting serious about Beau. I thought he was getting serious about me. I didn't understand he was marriage-phobic until that night."

"I'm not. I just—"

"I get it. You're not the marrying kind. That's fine. Since I would like to get married someday, we have no future. I'm glad I found that out before I got in any deeper."

"Jess, I'm not *phobic.*"

"Be honest with yourself, Beau, you're terrified of the idea. When the subject came up, you told me exactly how you viewed it. I got the message. Moving on."

"But what if my brother could change?" Angie's blue eyes filled with sisterly concern. "I've been watching him, and he cares about you. Little sisters know these things. Maybe you two could—"

"I don't think so, Angie." Jess hated crushing her hopes, but she wasn't willing to take a chance that Beau would break her heart a second time.

"But—"

"Beau flat-out told me he doesn't believe in marriage. I choose to believe him."

Angie's focus shifted from her to Beau. "Is that true?"

"No."

"There, see? He's—"

"But I'm wary, sis."

Some of the wind went out of Angie's sails, but she clearly wasn't defeated. "Wary isn't so bad, is it, Jess? We're talking about a lifetime commitment, here."

"Caution is good, but—"

"That's all Beau is talking about. Right, Beau?"

"Right."

"Those jokes sounded as if he'd never consider the idea."

Angie held his gaze. "Are you dead-set against it, big brother?"

"No."

"I didn't think so. Would you like to spend some time with the mother of your child and see if you can repair the damage?"

He turned to Jess and held her gaze. "Yes, I would."

"Would you consider that, Jess?"

Beau's little sister should consider offering her services to broker peace in the Middle East. "I'll... I'll think about it."

"Awesome!" Angie hugged her. "Thank you. We need to toast! Does everyone have drinks? We need more drinks!"

"I'll get 'em." Clint headed for the kitchen. "My job."

"I'll wrangle more snacks," Marybeth said.

"I'll help you guys." Beau took off like he'd been shot out of a cannon.

Angie laughed. "He hated being on the hot seat like that."

"I wasn't all that fond of it, myself."

"Sorry. It's a family tradition to have witnesses to an agreement. That way, the two people can't weasel out of it."

"I haven't agreed to do it."

"But you've agreed to think about it. And once you do, you'll probably—"

"No promises, Angie. Please don't get your hopes up."

She gave Jess a look far wiser than her years. "My hopes are always up."

Time to change the subject. "I guess being manager of the Buffalo is why Clint's in charge of drinks."

"Exactly." Angie pulled a hair tie out of her pocket and in seconds had tamed her unruly curls into a neat twist at the back of her head. "I love going in these days, especially now that Rance is bartending. Don't you, Bret?"

"Yeah, it's fun." A soft-spoken cowboy with arresting gray eyes, Bret co-owned a farrier business with his brother Gil. Both men had the muscles their profession required. "I'm glad you'll consider giving my brother another chance, Jess. He's a good guy at heart. He just doesn't always think before he speaks."

"I totally agree. Has business picked up for you and Gil? Last time we talked you said it was slow."

"Still pretty slow. We've found an alternate way to use our equipment to bring in some income. We're making ornamental gates and such."

"Brilliant."

"Turns out we like it, so that's a bonus."

"You know what? It would be an interesting feature story for the *Sentinel*. Would you be up for an interview? The publicity could bring you some extra business."

"I hadn't thought of that. Good idea. I'll let Gil do the talking though. He's better at it. Anyway, just wanted to say thanks. And good luck with that little kid."

She couldn't resist. "Which one?"

He blinked. Then he laughed. "Both." He glanced at the fireplace. "If you'll excuse me, I need to stoke up the fire. That's *my* job." He walked over and moved the grate aside.

Clearly Beau's family recognized his flaws and loved him anyway. They could afford to. She didn't have that luxury.

"Feature stories are good publicity, huh?" Angie's voice startled her out of her musing. She glanced to one side and discovered Beau's sister hadn't moved an inch from the territory she'd staked out at the epicenter of the action.

"They can be if it's an interesting story."

"Personally, I think my business is an interesting story."

"You have a business?"

"I started it the first of the year. Quit my job at Miller's Hardware."

"I wondered why I haven't seen you in there recently."

"Customers were always asking me to come out and help with their projects or repairs in my free time, so I thought, why not make it a business? It's called *The Fix-It Girl*. I'm a handywoman."

"That's great! But why didn't you head out with Buck to help with that leak?"

"Buck asked, because I'm good with finding leaks, but Mom wanted me to stay here. She said the male-female ratio wasn't great to start with and it would be worse without me. She values my input."

"I can see why." Angie was a game changer.

"Do you think my business is worth a story?"

Jess smiled. "You bet. I'll have to interview Bret and Gil first, but I'll work you in as soon as I can."

"You should wait a while, though. That'll give me more time to build up my client list. And you don't want anyone to think you're favoring the McLintocks."

"Good point."

"We have drinks and we have snacks." Clint arrived bearing a large tray crowded with bottles and Beau came behind him with bowls of fragrant popcorn and more chips.

"I made cheese puffs." Marybeth carried in two platters mounded with golf-ball-sized pastries fried to a golden brown.

In unison, the group cried out *cheese puffs* and descended on Marybeth.

All except Angie, who clearly had appointed herself Jess's sidekick. "Everyone loves Marybeth's cheese puffs. I'll elbow my way in and snag you some."

She pasted on a smile even though she had zero appetite. "Great!"

"Be right back." She returned in seconds with a small plateful. "Have one now, while they're still warm. That's when they're the best."

She popped one in her mouth to satisfy Angie. The burst of cheesy goodness caught her by surprise. "*Mmm.*"

"I like the sound of that." Beau's voice was close, very close. "Remind me to ply you with cheese puffs every chance I get."

His murmured words sent a shiver of excitement up her spine. Turning, she gazed into warm brown eyes filled with an emotion that tugged at her heart. She was well-acquainted with his teasing glances and his lustful ones. But he'd never looked at her with undisguised longing.

Had he missed her? Had she left a hole in his life when she'd ended their relationship? That didn't fit her image of him. He hadn't started dating again, though. In a town the size of Wagon Train, she'd know if he had.

As the crowd reassembled, Desiree tapped on her cider bottle with a spoon. "Before we get settled, we have one more item on the agenda. This new development means it's time to introduce Jess to M.R. Morrison."

"I already know who he is."

"Oh?" Desiree's eyebrows lifted and she glanced at Beau, who shook his head.

"Mom gave me one of his books years ago. I haven't kept up with all of them, but—"

"Let me rephrase. It's time for you to meet M.R. Morrison in person."

"Um, okay. That would be nice. Maybe I could interview him for the *Sentinel*." Jess glanced at her in confusion. "But I don't understand what he has to do with me becoming part of the family."

"Jess, *I'm* M.R. Morrison."

She blinked. "What?"

"I'm the author. M.R. Morrison is my pen name."

Clapping a hand to her mouth, she stared at Desiree as all the pieces fell into place—the prosperous ranch, the Western naming convention, the bookstore that always displayed the latest M.R. Morrison release in the front window.

"I'm trusting you, just as I trusted your mother, not to tell anyone, especially your father."

"My mom knew about this?"

"All the Wenches do. They're my beta readers."

"Oh, my gosh." Stunned, she gazed at Desiree, then scanned the crowded living room. "You've all kept this secret for almost thirty *years*? How is that even possible?"

Beau smiled. "Because we're just that good." That got a few laughs and a *hell, yeah* from Rance.

"I'm surprised it hasn't come out by now," Desiree said. "But the kids have been great about it. The Wenches, too. It's almost like a game. How much longer can we pull this off?"

"Are you sure my dad doesn't know? I can't believe my mom didn't tell him."

"I would have known if she had. Your father can't hide his emotions worth a damn."

"So true. I love that about him." She took a deep breath. "I promise not to be the weak link in the chain, but just so I know, what's at stake if word gets out?"

"It might not matter so much these days, but when I started, all the best-selling Western writers were men. My publisher advised me to choose a pen name that sounded masculine. I picked mine in honor of Marion Robert Morrison, aka John Wayne."

"Huh. I didn't make that connection. Clever."

"The M.R. Morrison personae grew from there. Reviewers began referring to the author as *he* because evidently I write like a man, whatever that means. I don't know what the fallout would be if the secret's revealed, but the books are selling great. I figure if it ain't broke, don't fix it."

"Where's your office? Or do you work in the library?"

"I have a gorgeous office. Would you like to see it?"

Oh, yeah. "If you don't mind."

"Not at all. It's a mess right now, but...Beau, why don't you take her back there while we get dinner on the table?"

"Be glad to." He put down his plate of cheese puffs.

"Don't touch anything, especially the computer. I think I saved what I did today, but this baby news has distracted me a bit. I might not have."

"We'll be careful. Come on, Jess. I'll show you where the magic happens."

"Just show her Mom's magic, lover boy," Sky said. "Leave your magic outside the door."

That made everybody grin.

"Hey." Beau glared at his siblings.

"Just sayin', bro."

"I just got a text from Buck." Marybeth tapped on her phone. "He and Lucky are on their way but it might take a while. The storm's a humdinger."

Beau gave Jess an I-told-you so look.

She'd been so engrossed in the goings-on inside that she'd missed the mixture of sleet and snow swirling outside the living room windows.

"Tell them to take their time," Desiree said. "And to holler if they get stuck. We'll send out the cavalry."

Marybeth tapped on her phone. "Done. I need volunteers for kitchen duty. We'll eat as soon as they get home."

Most everyone volunteered except Beau, who placed a warm hand at the small of her back. He pointed to a closed door. "That way."

"The library? She said that wasn't—"

"That's the anteroom to her office."

"I was in there for the interview. There's only one way in and out."

"Not quite true." He opened the door and ushered her in.

"My brain's still whirling. Morrison's written... what, at least forty books?

"The one she's working on will make it fifty-one."

"She wrote fifty books while she was raising ten kids?"

"She wrote faster and felt more creative when she was pregnant. She discovered that when she was working on her first one, when she was carrying Sky."

"Being pregnant inspired her to write a book?"

"Not exactly. Remember when I went to Apple Grove with my mom and Sky back in December?"

"Sure. To meet the widow of Sky's dad and find out more about the guy."

"That was part of it. Sky's dad was also the person who encouraged Mom to write. To celebrate fifty books, she wanted to let his widow know how grateful she was for that encouragement."

She fit another piece into the puzzle. Her mom had given her the first book in the series when she was around ten. The hero's name was Skyler, Sky for short. She'd thought it was a coincidence that she knew a boy who was a grade ahead of her named Sky McLintock.

"As scan these shelves, I don't see any books by M.R. Morrison." It was a dream of a library, though — shelves lining every wall, a rolling ladder for top-level access, and comfy wingback chairs, each a different color of the rainbow.

"She figured that would be too much on the nose, so she keeps those in her office. She has foreign editions, hardback and paperback, audio, large print."

"You said this was the anteroom, but there's no..." Or wait. That would be so *cool*. "Does one of these bookcases revolve?"

He gestured to the far wall. "Push on it."

"Oh, boy." She hurried toward it as the kid in her hopped up and down with excitement. "I've *always* wanted to have a revolving bookcase."

"So has my mom. When she found someone she could trust to build it for her, she was beside herself. Couldn't wait for it to be done."

"Who did the work?"

"Angie's dad. He was a master carpenter."

"Was?"

"Died in a rollover soon after Angie was born. Tore us all up something terrible. We liked him a lot."

"What a shame." She put pressure on the shelf. The bookshelf moved slowly and smoothly on its axis.

Soft lamplight revealed a huge U-shaped desk littered with stacks of paper, reference books and magazines. A desktop computer was hooked up to a massive monitor. Desiree had turned everything off. Fingers crossed she'd saved her work before she did that.

Although the library was windowless, the office was not. The storm whipped the trees outside, making the fairy lights dance.

Jess turned back to him. "If she's trying to keep her office private, how come she has so many windows?"

"It's high tech privacy glass."

"Nice." The room contained more bookshelves, and most of the titles looked like non-fiction reference works. But four long shelves held copies of M.R. Morrison's books in various editions. Framed literary awards lined the walls, along with classic Western art by Remington and Russell.

A double door on one wall was closed. "What's through there?"

"My mom's suite—bedroom, bath, exercise room."

"Does she have an agent?"

"Yes, and she knows, but it's to her financial advantage to protect Mom's identity. Like Mom says, maybe it wouldn't matter these days, but she might lose readers."

"She must have told some people in Apple Grove if that trip was all about the fiftieth book. Wasn't that risky?"

"It was, but so far, so good."

Turning in a circle, Jess took in the hidden office, the opening to the incredible library on the other side of the revolving bookcase, and...Beau. "Must have been tough keeping this to yourself all these years."

"Not with most people. Mom's career is important to her. And to all of us. I wouldn't do anything that could potentially jeopardize that. But I really hated keeping it from you."

"Why?"

"It bothered me that you were missing a big part of the picture."

"Of your family?"

"That, and... me. All this—" He swept an arm around the office. "It's part of who I am."

"Have you read her books?"

"Are you kidding? All of us have. Every word. She brought us into the process as soon as we were old enough to understand. We discuss plots and characters at the dinner table. This is a family business. But I couldn't talk about it, which meant you could never really know me."

Surprising admission coming from him. And he was right. Now she had new questions to ask, new territory to explore. He'd spent thirty years in close interaction with a woman who probed the depths of human experience in her books.

That added another dimension to Beau McLintock, one that aroused her reporter's curiosity. Oh, hell, it aroused the rest of her, too. Might as well admit that the sexiest man she'd ever met had just taken it up a notch.

9

Beau sure did like the way Jess was looking at him. He'd meant every word of that speech. He'd wanted to make it ever since they'd started dating in November.

By accident, his sincere outpouring had evidently sounded the right note. Jess was clearly intrigued by his unusual family dynamic. And curious about his part in it, thank the Lord.

Ever since hitting puberty he'd longed to use his mother's fame to get girls. But that avenue had been blocked. Until now.

Was he willing to take advantage of the added glow his mom added to his appeal? Damn straight.

During the hours of drinking with his mom, Sky and Penny at the newly christened Rowdy Roost last night, one concept had dominated the conversation. If he wanted a say in the fate of the baby he and Jess had made, he had two choices — get on her good side or hire a lawyer.

Judging from the interest in her gaze, he'd made some progress toward Option One. But he had to be careful, because she turned him on six ways to Sunday. If he started thinking with his johnson, he could ruin everything.

The longer he stayed in cozy isolation with Jess, the more likely that became. He didn't want to kill the mood, but he forced himself to make the right suggestion. "We'd better get back to the group."

"Yes, definitely." She broke eye contact immediately and walked straight out of the office and into the library, moving fast.

"I didn't mean you had to peel out." He closed the bookcase wall and lengthened his stride to catch up with her. "You left skid marks."

She paused and turned back to him. "Remember what you said in the truck? About making a quick exit?"

"Yes, ma'am, but—"

"I had the urge to jump your bones just now."

That made him smile a little. "Glad to hear it."

"Of course I wouldn't actually do it. Totally inappropriate."

That made him smile a lot. "I wouldn't have let you. I would have saved you from yourself."

"You can say that now, but I saw the look in your eye. If I'd put the moves on you, you would have been toast, buster."

He moved closer, got in her face. "Would not."

"Would so, smartass." The light of battle lit her green eyes.

"I'm stronger than you think, lady."

"Oh, yeah?" She grabbed the back of his head, pulled him down and planted one on him.

The second her lips touched his, he surrendered. For two solid months, he'd dreamed about Jess's mouth. If she was offering, he was taking. He thrust his tongue deep.

And she began sucking on it. His cock surged to life and he pulled her in tight to let her know what was waiting for her if she was interested.

She moaned and pressed closer.

Ah, Jess.

"Hey, guys, our travelers are home safe and sound, so dinner's—oh! Never mind."

He lifted his head in time to catch a glimpse of Angie hurrying out the library door. "Damn."

"That was a mistake." Jess was breathing hard.

So was he. He gazed into her flushed face and gulped for air. "Was it?"

"You know it was." She dragged in a breath. "We have a serious issue to work out. Indulging ourselves in... in..."

"Hot sex?"

"For want of a better description."

"There's no better description for what happens between you and me, Jess."

"Whatever. If we let ourselves succumb to these urges, we'll only make this more—"

"You started it."

"Only because you're so—"

"Irresistible?"

"Maddening. You're maddening, Beau."

"And irresistible. Let the record show that *you* kissed *me*."

"Whatever. Angie came to get us. We need to go in there and join your family for dinner. Turn me loose."

"I believe you're the one with your hands shoved in my hip pockets."

"Oh." She jerked them free and backed away. "Sorry. Habit."

"I never told you how much I love that move. Once your hands are in my back pockets grabbing my ass, I know we're in for a good time."

"Muscle memory. I didn't mean—"

"Oh, yes, you did. I was there. You took advantage of my tongue, lady. A guy doesn't forget a thing like that." Or a woman like Jess. He'd almost convinced himself she wasn't that special. One kiss had proved she was exactly that special.

* * *

The leak in the bookstore had been repaired and Lucky used pictures taken on his phone to show that no books had been harmed in the process. Marsh showed up at the last minute, jubilant about a successful foaling. Dinner turned into a celebration of good fortune that improved Beau's mood considerably.

He got a kick out of Jess, who was full of questions about the house, the bookstore, and the seemingly impossible feat of keeping the big secret. But their pre-dinner hot kiss took up most of the space in his brain.

Buck had painted a grim picture of the road conditions between the ranch and town. Getting Jess back to her house could be dicey. Even if they made it, he might not be able to leave. That possibility had promise, though. In fact....

His mother tapped on her wine glass to get everyone's attention. "I just checked my weather app, folks, and the storm's let up a bit but it's predicted to come back even stronger shortly."

Buck unfolded his tall, gaunt frame from his chair. "I was about to mention that. Marybeth and I need to skedaddle. Fortunately, we only have to drive about five hundred feet."

"By all means take off before it gets any deeper out there."

"Then we'll do that." Marybeth pushed back her chair. "I baked a whole mess of brownies today. They're in the fridge."

"Pack up some for yourselves," his mom said. "And don't try to get over here in the morning until the kids have shoveled a path."

"We won't." Buck picked up his dishes. "Important thing is the critters. Whoever gets up first, start clearing a path to the barn so we can feed."

"Will do," Sky said.

The Weavers took their leave, and his mom turned back to her brood. "You're all adults and free to make your own decision, but even our friendly little ranch roads aren't safe tonight. The storm could start up any minute, now. I'd feel better if you—"

"Hot damn, a sleepover." Lucky's dark eyes sparkled. "I was hoping for this on the drive home."

Jess's features tightened in alarm. "Desiree, I understand your concern, but—"

"And I understand yours." His mom smiled at her. "Everybody has a room to go to except you."

"She can bunk in with me." Angie gave Jess a sly glance. "Unless you'd rather—"

"No!" She blushed. "Your room would be great. Thanks."

His mom nodded. "I was about to suggest that. I can loan you a nightgown. You'll even have your own bunk, such as it is." She rolled her eyes at Angie.

"Mom hates those old bunk beds, but I love 'em."

"Lord knows why."

"They have character, Mom. And history."

"And they're pug-ugly." She turned to Jess. "I bought them second-hand for Sky and Beau. You can imagine how beat-up they are after being passed down the ranks. But my darling daughter thinks—"

"Are you saying you want to get rid of those bunks?" Sky sat forward in his chair.

"Sure do. When Angie moved into her own cabin, I figured they'd be history. But she wants to keep them in the family."

"Then let me have 'em. Penny and I can use them for our kids."

"Aw, no fair, bro." Cheyenne frowned. "I love those bunks, too. I know you're the oldest, but no telling when you and Penny will have—"

"We're working on it."

Penny gave him an elbow in the ribs.

"Well, we are, and nobody else is even—"

"What about Bret and me?" Gil put down his beer. "We've logged as many hours in those bunks as anyone."

"The bunks should go to whoever has the first kid." Clint focused on Beau.

Rance grinned. "And that person is... wait for it... *Beau McLintock*! Come on down, Beau, and claim your dilapidated but highly sought-after bunk beds!"

Thanks for nothing, you guys. Beau checked to see how Jess was reacting to the offer of bunk beds for their unborn child. Her little smile told him she found this exchange entertaining. No help, there.

He cleared his throat. "Clearly Angie's still enjoying them whenever she sleeps over. I wouldn't dream of taking those beloved bunk beds away from our sentimental little sis unless I had an immediate use for them. Which I don't."

Angie smiled. "Thanks, Beau." Her voice dripped with honey. "You always were my favorite."

Sky sent an apologetic glance her way. "I wasn't planning to haul them off next week. I just thought—"

"Here's an idea." Might as well polish his favorite brother trophy while he was at it. "Since possession is nine-tenths of the law, and Angie is currently in possession of those bunks, seems to me she gets to decide who gets 'em."

"I was gonna say that exact thing, big brother. You beat me to it."

"Yeah," Lucky said, "but Mom bought them in the first place, so shouldn't she be the one to decide? I mean, just because Angie ended up with them, why should she—"

"I want no part of this." His mom threw up her hands. "I can't believe you're all squabbling over those miserable bunk beds. Jess, when you see them, you'll wonder what's wrong with these kids of mine."

"You must love us, though, Mom." Rance gave her a puppy-dog gaze. "Otherwise you'd send us out into the snow instead of inviting us to stay here tonight. Which reminds me, who's ready for a poker tournament after we clean up the dishes?"

A chorus of *I'm in* followed. Jess was one of the most enthusiastic. Surprising. Card games hadn't been in the mix when they'd dated.

Beau glanced at Sky. "Should we set up the table in Rowdy Roost?"

"In here makes more sense. The fire's going good and we'd have to build a new one in there."

Cheyenne shoved back his chair. "Rowdy Roost? Is that what we're calling the bar?"

"Beau came up with it last night," Sky said. "Mom likes it."

"I do, but I haven't ordered the sign yet. Anybody object?"

"I like it," Clint said. "Alliteration's good. And we sure won't confuse it with the Fluffy Buffalo."

"Why would we ever confuse it with the Buffalo?" Bret looked puzzled. "It's a public bar in town and this is a private bar at our house. Two totally different categories."

"I know, but they're both bars, and it's better if ours doesn't have an animal name, like the Racy Raccoon or the Cozy Coyote."

Rance laughed. "Those are good names, Clint. Don't tell them to anybody, okay? One of us might want to use them for something."

"I can't wait to see a business called the Racy Raccoon," Gil said. "I'd go in there regardless of what they were selling."

"Dude, you know what they'd be selling." Rance gave him a wink. "Remember that store we found in Helena? The one where they had the battery operated—"

"Boys, keep it classy." His mom circled the group with a quelling gaze. "We have a guest."

"Whoops." Rance focused on Jess. "Sorry, ma'am. I meant no offense."

"No offense taken. Those shops perform a valuable service. Not everyone has a partner."

Beau gulped. Not a topic he'd like discussed in his current situation. Did Jess avail herself of battery-operated gizmos? Damn, didn't need that image planted in his brain. "Did I hear somebody mention a poker tournament?"

"Hell, yeah. Let's move it." Clint pushed back his chair and stood, prompting everyone else to do the same and start clearing the table.

"I'll take Sam out." Marsh let out a soft whistle and the collie trotted down the hall after him.

"Out where?" Jess stared at Beau in confusion.

"There's a sheltered area around the side of the house by the woodshed. Sam will be okay. He's got his winter coat."

"I'm sure he will." She began collecting dishes. "But what about Marsh?"

"He's got his winter coat hanging by the front door." Beau gathered up several serving bowls. "And here's a secret about my brother. He's a little proudful about suffering right along with the animals. I think it's a vet thing."

"And I'll bet he's a good one." She started back to the kitchen. "I don't remember how cleanup works."

"That's because both times you had dinner here, I traded favors so we could leave early." Taking her back to his cabin instead of sharing kitchen duty was totally worth spit-shining all his brothers' dancing boots. At least it'd been a good trade-off on Yule. Christmas Eve, not so much.

"I hope your mom has a ginormous dishwasher."

"She has several."

Jess laughed. "I like that idea."

He and his siblings had kitchen duty down to a science. Sky gave Jess a task and she fit right into the routine. Had fun doing it, too, judging from her smiling face.

Setting up for poker was also engineered with military precision. When Jess got a glimpse of the ten-person poker table, her eyebrows rose. She sidled over in Beau's direction. "That's a serious-looking piece of equipment. It has recessed drink cups."

"We play a lot."

"It only has room for ten, though."

"We can squeeze everybody in, add a side table for drinks if necessary. Mom usually bails early."

"I see."

"Want to reconsider? You don't have to take part."

"Oh, no, I want to play."

He made eye contact and caught the gleam of battle. Well, then. "You're good, aren't you?"

The gleam grew brighter. "That's a relative term." She glanced toward Angie who was beckoning to her. "I think your sister wants to show me which bunk is mine. Be back in a minute." She sashayed away.

Chances were excellent Jess would kick his ass at this friendly little game. Clearly she had experience. And his focus would be shot to hell. In a few hours, she'd be sleeping two doors down from his room. And he wouldn't be able to do a thing about it.

_10_

Once the plan was in place, Jess called her father to let him know she wouldn't be out on the road tonight. He sounded relieved, offered to go over and feed her cat in the morning, and told her to have a good time.

Which she did. High on adrenaline, she'd never played better poker in her life. Being in the same room with Beau energized her — it always had. Being in the same bed doubled the charge. Not that she'd be sharing a bed with him tonight.

Evidently being in the same room with her had the opposite effect on his poker game. His meager stack of chips was unusual enough to inspire comment from his siblings. Typical Beau, he laughed it off.

As he'd predicted, Desiree cashed out early. "Be back in a sec." She left the table and headed for the library.

Now that Jess had been given a tour, that room took on a whole new meaning. The library gave Desiree a layer of privacy for her writing and the office added another layer to protect her personal life.

She returned with a red flannel granny gown she handed to Jess. "This is a one-size fits none, but it should work okay for tonight."

"Thank you. That's very kind."

"It's the least I can do since you're relegated to the bottom bunk of that pitiful bed."

"It'll be fine. Thanks for the nightwear."

"You're welcome." She surveyed her brood. "See you kids in the morning. We'll have some shoveling to do, so don't stay up too late." She smiled, gave Sam a soft command, and left the room. The collie followed her.

Clint chuckled. "Do you think she'll ever stop saying *don't stay up too late*?"

"Probably not." Sky gathered in the chips he'd won in the last round. "She has to know we'll ignore her and stay up as long as we damn well please. But she sees it as her job to remind us to be sensible."

Jess glanced around the table. "She's a terrific mom. Clearly she was meant for the role."

Beau gazed at her from his position at the far end of the table, one he'd likely chosen on purpose. "She wants to be there for you, too."

"I know, and that's very sweet. She said the Wenches would probably want to—"

"Oh, boy." Clint chuckled. "That'll be a dinner and a show."

"What do you mean?"

"For one thing, they still miss your mom. She left a hole."

"Tell me about it. I didn't feel the loss as much in Philadelphia, but this town is full of memories."

"For all of them, too," Clint said. "I predict they'll go nuts over this baby news. Somebody here might know different, but I don't think any of them has a grandchild yet."

Cheyenne nodded. "Mom would've been all over it if they had, buying baby gifts right and left. The Wenches will probably overreact, but the one who'll clean out the Baby Barn is Mom."

Uh-oh. "I don't want her doing that. Is there any way to nicely rein her in?"

"No." Beau and Sky spoke in unison.

"Maybe I can hold her back some." Angie shuffled the cards.

"Good idea," Penny said. "I volunteer to help you. We could tag along when she—"

"She'd go for that," Beau said. "Two extra pairs of hands to carry all the loot."

"Very funny. Penny and I make a good team. We'll be diplomatic about it. We'll just gently suggest that she doesn't have to buy the *entire* store."

"Since you're the baby in the family—"

Angie rolled her eyes. "Thanks, Sky. You know how much I love hearing that."

"I'm just pointing out that you've never seen her in newborn mode. I have. Repeatedly."

"Yeah, well, you were just a kid, then. Penny and I are mature women with attitude. We can handle her."

"And maybe you can," Sky said. "Personally, I'd let her go for it. She loves the process. Starting with Marsh, she really indulged her passion for baby stuff."

"She did?" He beamed. "You never told me that."

"Don't let it go to your head, bro."

"I'm totally letting it go to my head. I'm special."

"It's not you, dude," Beau said. "It's the royalties from her books. She finally had the money to splurge by the time you showed up. I helped her pack the hand-me-downs that Clint, Cheyenne and I wore. Also any toys we didn't want. I learned at an early age there were kids who didn't have that stuff."

Sky nodded. "Same here. I even gave away toys I liked because I decided those kids needed them more than me."

"That's sweet." Penny gave him a one-armed hug.

"I wasn't the only one. We've all done that at some point."

"It felt good, too," Beau said. "She taught us how nice it feels to be generous. Then she'd take us along when she shopped for the next baby. Nothing for us, because the baby needed fun stuff. We all got into the spirit of it."

"And then there was you, little sis." Clint and Cheyenne exchanged a glance. "Remember that, bro?"

"Sure do. The shopapalooza. What a haul."

"Really?" Angie stared at them in disbelief. "But she didn't spoil me when I was growing up."

"Oh?" Marsh lifted dark eyebrows. "What about Silky Boy?"

"Well, I suppose a Shetland pony is a luxury, but that's the only extravagant thing I can think of. She didn't take any of us on wild shopping sprees that I remember. If she splurged on my baby stuff, how would I know?"

"That's the point," Beau said. "I remember her saying when she took us shopping for Rance that you can't spoil a baby by treating him or her like a precious gift. That's how she felt about all of us." He looked down the table at Jess. "And clearly how she feels about this baby."

"So if I object to her overspending, I'll ruin something she loves doing?"

"Yes, ma'am."

She took a deep breath. "Okay." Then she smothered a yawn. "Sorry. I might have to cash in, too." She picked up the nightgown she'd been holding on her lap. Then she looked at her pile of chips. "Although that's not very sporting of me, is it?"

Sky laughed. "No worries. You earned every bit of that. Anyway, we should wrap this up so we can all hit the sack. We'll be clearing snow in the morning."

"I heard your mom say that, but it confused me. Don't you have a snowplow?"

"We do," Clint said, "but it's in the tractor barn. We have to shovel our way down to it, and a few of us head over and dig out Buck and Marybeth's place."

"Not that they couldn't do it themselves," Cheyenne said. "But when we're all here, why not?"

"So then you use the tractor to clear a path to the horse barn?"

"The plow's more for the ranch roads." Clint stacked his chips in neat piles. "The path to the horse barn is easy shoveling. Only about sixty yards, a two-person job. And it's the most fun because at the end you feed the critters."

"Sounds like you have a system."

"Yes, ma'am. Sky does. He's in charge of snow removal."

"I sure am, and the more we talk about it the more I want to get some sleep. Everybody count your chips and I'll divvy up the pot."

Jess tallied her winnings and pocketed a tidy sum. "Thanks, Sky." She tucked her borrowed nightgown under her arm.

"Nice job tonight. Where'd you learn to play?"

"A bunch of us from the station had a weekly game. It was fun even when I wasn't very good. Then I took lessons and it was even more fun."

"Well, it was a pleasure to lose to you, right, Beau?"

He smiled. "I'm so happy I could bust. You can keep my fifty-three cents, bro. Save it for the next time. Maybe Jess will give us a rematch."

"Are you inviting me to your next poker game?"

"If he doesn't, I will," Sky said. "You're a part of the family, now."

"Thank you."

Clint came over to collect his share of the pot. "Are you setting up a rematch with Jess? Because I'd sure like to have another shot at a game with this lady. I also see some poker videos in my future."

"I'm trying to set it up." Sky glanced at her. "What do you say?"

"Well, sure, okay. Just let me know when. I'll put it on my calendar."

"Great. I imagine we'll play after Angie's birthday party. You're invited to that, anyway."

"When is it?"

"I was born on Valentine's Day." Angie joined the group. "And you're definitely invited to my party. You don't have to get me anything. Just come."

"Uh-uh, I'm not coming to your birthday party empty-handed. Not after you've offered to let me sleep in your cherished bunk bed. Besides, thanks to this poker game, I'm loaded."

Beau chuckled. "Yeah, yeah. Rub it in. Me, I'll have to take out a loan to buy my little sis a gift."

"You're ridiculous." Angie punched him on the arm. "And you don't have to buy me anything, either. I'm twenty-four."

"Not yet, sis."

"In seven days. The point is, at this age I don't need presents. I just want a big ol' party."

"I'm still getting you something," Jess said. "I'll have fun doing that. In a way, I understand your mom's urge to shop for baby stuff. I love buying gifts, too."

"I can give you some tips for Angie." Beau waggled his eyebrows. "But we need to sneak off to a corner so she can't hear us."

Jess smiled. "All right." Sounded innocent enough. She put her borrowed nightgown on the arm of the leather sofa.

"Come with me." He took her hand and led her toward the arched doorway on the far side of the dining room.

"Wait, where are we going?" As if she didn't know. Through that arch was a hallway. A right would take them to the kitchen. A left and they'd soon be in the sleeping quarters. Not so innocent, after all.

"My room."

She tugged him to a halt. "That's a bad idea."

"Angie has ears like a bat. We have to get out of range or she'll hear every word we say." He gave her a coaxing glance and lowered his voice. "Don't worry. I'm not going to seduce you."

"Yes, you are."

"Have I ever lied to you?"

She battled the fizzy sensation that threatened to derail her good sense. "You said you weren't *going to* seduce me — future tense. Technically true. The seduction's already begun."

"I don't know what you're talking about."

"You're stroking my palm with your thumb. You know that gets me hot."

His eyes widened in pretend surprise. "It does?"

"*Beau.*" She tried to pull her hand free but he tightened his grip.

"I promise we'll keep every stitch of our clothes on."

"That leaves a lot of wiggle room."

He grinned. "Nicely put."

"It's a figure of speech."

"One of my favorites. Great name for a strip club. Not that I frequent those, but if someone had the creativity to name a place *The Wiggle Room* I just might have to consider patron—"

"We're way off-topic. Are you going to give me gift ideas for your sister or not?"

He sighed. "That was a smokescreen. I need to talk to you privately about something super important. I have an idea."

"You always do. And it usually involves hanky-panky."

"Well, you've got me there. This idea does involve hanky-panky. Not now, though. Later on. Future tense."

"I don't want that."

"Yes, you do. You just think it's a mistake."

She had no response. When he was right, he was right.

"Just give me ten minutes."

The words triggered instant recall of the day he'd met her for lunch and talked her into going to her house for a quickie. *Just give me ten minutes.* He'd accomplished a lot in that time.

She took a steadying breath. "I'll go with you if you'll turn my hand loose and promise you'll maintain your distance. No touching."

"You drive a hard bargain, lady." He released her. "I promise. We're off." As he started down the hall, he pulled out his phone. "In the spirit of cooperation, I'm setting a ten-minute alarm."

"Good." He'd set one that day, too. His timing had been impeccable. And thrilling. Damn, she was turning herself on. The Beau McLintock effect.

He paused in front of an open door to a room that was right across from Angie's.

Had she known that when Angie had taken her back there earlier, she would have peeked in.

Reaching through the doorway, he flipped a wall switch for the lights. "After you."

She walked and looked around. It was a typical boy's room, with sports posters and a couple of pinups on the wall.

Some items weren't so typical, though. An impressive dragon kite hung from the ceiling. Instead of books, his bookshelves were stuffed with unusual objects, enough of them that only the bigger ones stood out—a hefty German beer stein, a model of the Eiffel Tower, a decorated boomerang, a giant nutcracker.

She gazed up at the kite's brilliant colors. "Is that silk?"

"Yes, ma'am."

"Where did you—"

"We can talk about that later. Would you like to sit on the bed?"

"I'll stand, thanks."

"Okay." He closed the door.

Immediately the atmosphere in the room heated. She'd never been alone with him in a bedroom without clothes coming off. She swallowed. "What's this idea?"

"I want you to live with me for a week, until Angie's birthday."

"*Live* with you? Are you nuts? I don't plan to go out with you again, let alone live in your cabin."

"Oh, yeah, dating is absolutely out. No point. That's what I was into last December, because I thought of us as two separate people."

"Which we *are*. This baby doesn't change that. I'll have my life and you'll have yours. Clearly your family wants me around and that will be even more true once the baby's born, but I won't be here to see you."

"Yes, you will."

"Honestly, you're the most egotistical—"

"Come on, Jess. You're attracted to me and—"

"I'm planning to fix that."

"I'm attracted to you and I have no intention of fixing it."

"That's your business."

"And yours. Fighting an attraction to me won't be easy when I keep giving you the look."

"The *look*? Oh, please." Her voice wasn't quite steady. Neither was her heartbeat.

"Pretend all you want. You said it turns your knees to rubber."

"Back then it did. Not now."

"And made your panties damp."

"I can control that reaction." She'd keep telling herself that.

"Good luck keeping your cool. I sure can't. I predict the more we're together at these friendly family gatherings, the more frustrating those occasions will become. For both of us."

"Don't assume that. They say familiarity breeds contempt."

"Then you should be all over my plan. The more we're together, the sooner you'll get over me."

Or I could end up hopelessly in love with the wrong guy. "Why are you suggesting this crazy thing? What do you hope to prove?"

He took a deep breath. "That I can change."

11

Beau slowly let the air seep from his lungs. Jess wasn't buying it. Doubt showed in her expression and every tense muscle in her tempting body. Her rigid, protective stance cut him to the quick. He'd inspired her behavior with a few careless comments on Christmas Eve.

The clock was ticking, so he set to work. "I never wanted to be a father. I was horrified when you told me."

"I know."

"That didn't last long, but you were gone before the shock wore off. What was left was a rock-solid determination. I want to be a real father, a significant part my baby's life."

She swallowed. "Meaning what, exactly?"

"I want you to trust me when it comes to our kid. At this point you probably wouldn't."

"Maybe not, but I'd count on your mom to make sure—"

"See, that's exactly what I'm talking about. I want you to trust me. Not my mother, not my extended family. *Me.*"

"But you just admitted you never wanted to be a father. Why should I—"

"I'm getting to that. I spent most of last night talking with Mom, Sky and Penny. They reluctantly agreed that I don't come off as a responsible dad type. I'm more the fun-loving uncle who'll let 'em eat all the candy they want and stay up long past their bedtime."

"I'd go along with that evaluation."

There it was. Out in the open. She didn't believe their baby would be safe in his hands. His fault, but it hurt, all the same. "All my life I've figured I'd be that uncle, but life didn't work out that way. I need to recalibrate."

"In a week? Nobody can—"

"Of course not. But I can get a start on it. If you're there with me, you can see that I'm making a genuine effort to think before I speak, to crack a few less jokes, to admit I'm not the coolest dude on this ranch..." He paused, gave a shrug.

"You're saying it like we'll be spending every moment together. I have a job. You have clients."

"Not at night."

"Aha. I know where this is going. You're not looking for a platonic roommate, then?"

"Well, no, I wasn't thinking that, exactly."

"I'm so surprised."

"This transformation needs to include my approach to sex."

Her eyelids fluttered. "Do tell."

Thank God for that eyelash flutter. It was a tell. She wasn't over him. "There again, my emphasis has been on fun and games. Making you come as many times as possible."

Her breath caught and her pupils widened.

If he hadn't promised not to touch her… but he had promised, and besides, finding a way to have sex with her tonight would be something the old Beau would do.

The new Beau still wanted to, but he'd forgo short-term pleasure for long-term gain. "I want to transition from having sex to making love." He gave her the look. Because it worked, damn it. And he was fighting for his life, his life as the father of the baby they'd made.

Pressing her hand to her chest, she backed toward the door. "I'll… I'll think about it."

"And let me know in the morning?"

She nodded. Turning, she fumbled with the knob and wrenched the door open.

He gave her time to escape. When he walked into the hall, the door to Angie's room was shut. Dollars to donuts Jess was on the other side of that door, breathing hard, eyes closed as she wrestled with the emotions he'd stirred up.

He took in a few lungsful of air, himself. Then he sauntered over to the door, Steve McQueen style, and tapped on it.

"Go away."

"My time's not up."

"I'm not coming out."

"I figured. A gift certificate to Miller's Hardware."

"What?"

"Angie will love that."

"Oh. Thanks."

"You're welcome." His alarm went off and he silenced it. "Sleep tight." Turning away, he made for the living room, likely to give a report.

Yep. Every one of his siblings was still there. Penny, too. Ten pairs of eyes focused on him.

"Well?" Cheyenne spoke first, his blue gaze intent. "Did she kick you out?"

"For your information, we parted amicably."

"Then where is she?" Rance leaned forward. "If you two are so amicable, why didn't she come back out with you?"

"She's tired. She's probably in bed by now."

Clint's blue eyes, identical to his twin's, sparkled. "Yours or hers?"

"Hers."

Angie picked up the red nightgown Jess had left on the arm of the sofa. "If your parting was amicable, she would have come back to get this."

Lucky sighed. "Good point, sis. From the look of things, our big brother didn't convince Jess to give him another chance."

"I didn't, but that doesn't mean—"

"It means she hasn't changed her mind about you." Gil pointed the neck of his beer bottle in Beau's direction. "You're gonna have to try harder, bro. A lot rides on her liking you again."

"I know. That's why I asked her to come live with me for the next week."

Clint groaned. "And you think that'll work?"

"Worked for me." Sky grinned, clearly delighted. "I win. That's the way I bet. I figured you'd take a page out of my playbook."

"So you were all out here taking bets? That's so..." He shook his head and chuckled, in spite of himself. "So Rowdy Ranch."

"Sky's the only one who guessed it," Rance said. "I bet on you keeping her in your room tonight and convincing her that way."

"Me, too," Clint said. "Along with Gil, Lucky and Penny."

"Penny?" Beau turned to her. "You thought I'd try to seduce her in a house full of family members?"

"Can you blame me? I've been getting an earful of your escapades ever since I moved here. You have quite the reputation."

"Yes, ma'am. I'm aware." He rubbed the back of his neck. "And I have a favor to ask. If you could all put a lid on those stories, you'd help my cause."

"That's what I've been saying, bro." Marsh looked around the group. "We should work on fixing your image and you need to do some serious groveling."

"Groveling?" He didn't like the sound of that.

"Yessir. Bret, Cheyenne and I put our money on you throwing yourself at her feet and begging her to date you again."

He winced. "That's not exactly my style."

"Desperate times, dude. Desperate measures."

"I agree, but dating's the wrong way to go. We need constant contact so I can show her I'm capable of being a responsible dad."

"You are." Angie held his gaze. "You just need to straighten up."

Straightening up was a damn sight better than groveling. "You're right, sis."

"Of course I'm right. What did Jess say when you asked her to move in for a week?"

"That she'd think about it."

"Yes!" Angie pumped a fist in the air. "I should get half the pot, Sky. I bet on him asking to work this out and her saying she'd think about it."

"I'll split it with you if you'll forgive me for trying to steal those bunks."

"Deal." She looked at Beau. "Why did you choose my birthday as the deadline for this moving-in experiment?"

"Because it's—*hello*—Valentine's Day. I'll spend the whole week being my best self, convincing her I'm daddy material. Your birthday will seal the deal because it's such a fun family occasion. She likes this family. It's me she's worried about."

Sky gazed at him. "Seal the deal? Does that mean what I think it does?"

He grew uneasy. "Probably not."

"You aren't planning to propose at the end of this live-in?"

"Too quick."

Penny glanced at him. "It wasn't for your big brother."

"But you turned him down, as I recall?"

"I did, but I changed my mind when I realized the length of time was less important than the depth of feeling." She snuggled into the crook of Sky's arm. "And I've never regretted making that decision."

"I thought you chose a week on purpose," Sky said, "because a week was the perfect timing for Penny and me."

"No, it was just the Valentine's Day thing and Angie's birthday. I thought the plan needed a beginning and end. Asking her to live with me for some unspecified time... she wouldn't have gone for it."

Sky gave him a knowing look. "And neither would you."

His big brother knew him too damn well. It was disconcerting. "Probably not, when it comes to that."

"Then I have a question." Bret cleared his throat. The quietest of the brothers, he didn't speak up often, but when he did, everybody paid attention. "If you're not going to propose, what is your end game?"

"That's easy. I want Jess to trust me to be a good father. I want her to be fine with me teaching this kid to ride and play baseball and camp out, and—"

"So getting on her good side is just a means to an end?" Bret frowned. "Because that's not a very noble—"

"Sure isn't," Beau said. "Especially when you put it that way. I didn't say it right. I want to create a solid relationship with Jess. I don't have that, now, and I'm not happy about it."

"Do you love her?" Angie pinned him with a stare and waited.

He began to sweat. "I do, but—"

Angie gave a whoop of joy. "I knew it!"

"If you tell her, I—"

"I won't. She needs to hear it from you, not me."

His shoulders sagged in relief. "The thing is, we're not there yet, sis."

"You will be." She gave him the smug smile of inexperience.

"I just need everyone to know I'm not ready to propose. For now, I want her to agree that we'll raise our kid together. That means I have to mend some fences if I want to be considered an equal partner."

"Why not do it gradually?" Bret studied him, concern in his gray eyes. "Why set up a week of forced togetherness where something is bound to go wrong? Seems kind of hare-brained to me."

"Gradual isn't my strong suit." And he needed to play to his strengths. But unlike the rabbit in *The Tortoise and the Hare*, he would make sure he crossed the finish line of this race.

<u>12</u>

Faint murmurs from the conversation going on in the living room drifted down the hall, but Jess couldn't make out any of it. Even after she opened the door a crack, she couldn't understand the gist of what was being discussed.

Then again, the content was a given. The retreating click of Beau's boot heels as he'd walked back down the hall told her he'd gone to rejoin his family in the living room. Would he tell them what he'd asked her to do? Given the openness within this family, he likely would.

She flopped down on the bottom bunk to wait for Angie, who would likely bring the red nightgown. Sleeping in her clothes, or even in her underwear, held no appeal, so she'd hang out until the group packed it in for the night.

That left her with nothing to do but review the current situation. She shouldn't give Beau's audacious request a second thought, let alone give it serious consideration. Living out here and working at the *Sentinel* would be a gigantic pain in the ass. She'd lose more than an hour a day commuting.

On top of that, she'd have to give up her twice-weekly dinners with her dad. She'd have to pack up a week's worth of clothes and cart them out to Beau's cabin. She'd spent the night there several times, but staying for days was a whole other ball of wax involving toothbrushes and cooking, and—

What about the cooking? No restaurants out here. Like all Desiree's kids, Beau could handle himself in the kitchen. But they'd be preparing meals together every night. It would be a routine, not a special occasion. What would that be like?

She had zero experience living with a guy. Or anyone other than her parents. In college she'd had her own apartment. Same in Philadelphia.

Why was she even thinking about taking him up on his request? She wasn't going to do it. Sure, she'd had some daydreams back in December about living out here. She'd romanticized it as an adventure. Driving into town and back every day would allow her to soak up the beauty of the Montana countryside.

But Beau hadn't suggested that this week was a trial run that could lead to moving in together permanently. He hadn't mentioned marriage at all, although he'd committed himself to being an involved dad.

She hadn't figured on that. Or on how much she'd be charmed and fascinated by his family and their well-kept secret. If she stayed here beginning tomorrow, the time would include a weekend when she wouldn't have to go to work.

Another chat with Desiree would be fun. Maybe some of the Wenches would come by on the weekend. Now she'd be in on the secret, so she could—

A light tap on the door followed by Angie's *can I come in?* brought her upright so fast she bumped her head on the springs of the top bunk. "Ouch."

"Oh, no." Angie opened the door. "You banged your head. I forgot to warn you how easy that is to do when you're an adult."

"And an adult who's never slept in a bunk bed." Jess rubbed the top of her head. "But I didn't hit it very hard. I'm fine."

"You've never slept in one?" Angie came the rest of the way in and closed the door.

"Amazing, isn't it? But my room at home had two twins in case I had anybody over, and none of my friends had bunks, either. I always thought they were cool, though. Easy-peasy to make a hideout. I had to use a card table."

"Yeah, this bed has kept me safe from train robbers, rustlers, even Billy the Kid."

Jess laughed. "You can't let your mom give it away."

"After that ruckus tonight, she wouldn't dare." She handed over the nightgown. "Bathroom's the door on the left. You can be first. Extra towels are in the cupboard along with a new toothbrush."

"I hate to use that for only one night."

"Please do. It's your souvenir. Mom keeps all the bathrooms supplied with new ones."

"Do you have a lot of overnight visitors?"

"Off and on."

"How in the world do you keep your mom's secret from them?"

"Since the visitors are often one of the dads, they already know."

"They don't stay with her?" Then she caught her breath. "Forget I asked. None of my business."

"Now it is your business, and no, they don't. Once a dad leaves Rowdy Ranch, the sexual part of the relationship is over. They're welcome to come back and visit but no funny business. I sometimes think the ones who've never come back, like Beau's dad, stay away because they really fell for her and they're steering clear, now."

"He's *never* visited?"

"Nope. But he's sent a ton of gifts to Beau."

"Like the dragon kite?"

"Isn't it amazing? I've tried to get my brother to fly that thing, which is its purpose, after all, but he won't risk it."

Her throat tightened. Inside that big ol' cowboy was a little boy who didn't want to ruin his father's gift or part with a single treasure from that mysterious globe-trotter. "Have you told Beau your theory about why his dad doesn't visit?"

"No, because I could be wrong, and besides, he doesn't like to talk about it."

"I can understand that." Made her chest hurt, too.

"Listen, Jess, I promised myself I wouldn't pester you, but I can't help it. Are you gonna do this one-week experiment?"

"Yes." She took a deep breath. "Please keep it to yourself, but yes, I believe I am."

* * *

Jess had barely closed her eyes when several pairs of boots clomping in the hallway woke her up. She picked up her phone from the floor beside her bed. Six in the morning. How had that happened?

Angie's long legs appeared over the edge of the top bunk. She slid noiselessly to the floor and began dressing in the dark.

"You don't have to be quiet, Angie. I'm awake."

"Yeah?" She turned toward the bed as she zipped her jeans. "Wanna come out and help shovel?"

"Love to."

Angie laughed. "It was a joke. You're a guest. You don't have to—"

"I'm not a guest anymore. I'm family. And family pitches in."

"Alrighty, then." She sounded pleased. "Glad to have you."

"I might need to borrow some rubber boots if they're available." She swung her sock-covered feet to the floor and sat up carefully so she wouldn't hit her head again.

"We keep extra barn boots in the entryway closet."

"Great."

"Oh, and I have a spare parka you can wear." She moved to the closet and slid back the door. Hangers rattled as she pulled out a coat and tossed it over to the bed. "Your green wool is too nice for shoveling."

"I could make it work."

"Nah, use mine. It's old. And there's a pair of work gloves in the pocket."

"Okay. Thanks."

"You know what? That sweater you wore last night is too nice for this kind of job." She rummaged in the closet and threw Jess a flannel shirt. "Put that on, instead. I'm guessing we're about the same size."

"Do you normally keep extra clothes here?"

"Just the ratty ones, so you won't win any fashion contests in that shirt. But nobody cares, especially the horses. I'll bet Sky will assign you and Beau to the barn path. He's a romantic just like me."

"So we'd be alone on that path?"

"That's the idea. I shouldn't promise you'll get that assignment, but I hope you do. It's great to see how happy the horses are when you get there. Oh, and the pigs."

"Beau moved the pigs to the barn?"

"He does that whenever a big storm is predicted. No way would he leave Slim and Pickens if he thinks he might end up here overnight."

"I'm glad to hear it." She'd forgotten about the pigs but evidently Beau never did. Another sign he might not be as irresponsible as he seemed.

"I'll take first shift in the bathroom while you get dressed." She whisked out the door.

Jess tugged on her jeans and slid her arms into the soft flannel shirt. Instantly she felt more like a ranch girl. She didn't own any flannel shirts, let alone old ones like this that had been broken in. Even her borrowed nightgown hadn't been this cozy.

Quickly fastening the buttons, she tucked the shirttail into her jeans and padded over to the shadowy bulk of a highboy dresser. The lamp on top provided the only light except the overhead and she wasn't awake enough for the overhead.

She pulled the chain, filling the wood-paneled room with a warm glow. Then she blinked. Her reflection stared back at her from the full-length mirror attached to the adjacent wall. Darned if she didn't look like a cowgirl, too. The faded green plaid was a hundred times more authentic than any rhinestone-studded shirt in the window of Hannigan's Western Wear.

"Hey, that suits you." Angie walked back in. "You should keep it."

"Can I?" She was ridiculously happy about the offer. "I can't imagine why I don't own any. But even if I get some now, they won't feel like this."

"That's the truth. It takes a couple of years to get them softened up, but the good news is, I've been collecting flannel shirts ever since I stopped growing, around eighteen. I'm embarrassingly overstocked. You need to take a few."

She gazed at Angie. "Seriously?"

"Seriously. I promise I'm not trying to bribe you, either. Please know that even if things don't work out with Beau—"

"What do you mean, *work out*?"

"Full disclosure, I'm hoping you two end up getting married."

Jess swallowed. "That's not likely. A solid friendship would be great, though."

"And maybe you'll end up in friends-with-benefits territory. But I think you're in love with my brother."

"Well, I—"

"You don't have to confirm or deny. I just know what I saw on your face when you found out he won't risk flying the dragon kite. If that wasn't love, then put me on Silver and call me the Lone Ranger."

<u>*13*</u>

To his surprise, Beau slept well. He'd followed Angie back to the bedroom wing, and the sound of his sister and Jess talking behind the closed door of Angie's room had soothed him. The conversation was muffled and impossible to decipher, but his baby sis was on his side. He couldn't have a better ally. Having Jess spend the night in Angie's room might help his cause a whole lot.

Out of habit, he was awake before six, dressed soon after and joining his brothers in a march down the hall. Showers and shaving would happen later, after they'd accomplished the task.

He and Sky ended up leading the group headed to the kitchen, where traditionally they grabbed a cup of coffee before tackling the mounds of snow. He glanced at Sky. "Penny's not coming to shovel?"

"Are you kidding? She was up earlier than me. That coffee you smell is her doing."

"I thought maybe Mom was up."

"She might be. I just know Penny was moving fast this morning and offered to go start the coffee."

"Nice of her."

"She's the best."

"Hey, did she put in some cinnamon rolls, too? Because I could swear—"

"She'd wait for Mom before doing that. Mom must be up." Sky glanced at him. "What about Jess? Think she'll come out and help?"

"Probably. She's not the type to sit on the sidelines."

"I like that about her."

"Yeah, me, too." If she joined in, would Sky assign the two of them to the barn path? That possibility wiped the sleep cobwebs from his brain right quick.

He stepped into the warm, fragrant kitchen where Penny was lining up mugs on the counter. His mom had just pulled the second cookie sheet of rolls out of the oven and Sam was gobbling up the food in his bowl. Jess wasn't there. Not yet, anyway.

"Oh, boy, cinnamon rolls!" Angie's happy cry came from the hallway.

His heart rate picked up. His little sis wouldn't be making that much noise if her roommate was still asleep.

Was Jess with her? Turning to peer down the hall was a doofus move, so he focused on the activity in the kitchen. His brothers had already surrounded the oversized coffee pot, jockeying for a chance to get their first cup.

"Ladies, this is heaven." Clint came over to the stove and helped himself to a roll from the cookie sheets their mom had placed on top of it. "Thank you."

"You're welcome, but use a saucer, son." She held one out. "You're dropping crumbs."

"Thanks, Mom. Although Sam would appreciate those crumbs."

"Ah, cinnamon rolls." Clint's twin put one on a saucer from the stack on the counter. "Reminds me I need to start making them at the firehouse."

"You guys can thank your mom for remembering to take them out of the freezer last night," Penny said.

"Appreciate it, Mom." Angie sang out as she came into the kitchen, Jess behind her.

He couldn't help it. He looked right at her and to his surprise she looked right back. Her warm smile turned his insides to melted butter.

Sky asked Cheyenne something about the firehouse, but Beau had checked out of that conversation. Jess's smile commanded all his attention. Was he imagining the happy glow in her eyes?

She wore a faded flannel shirt, one of Angie's old ones. What a transformation. The sophistication she'd acquired in the big city had been spellbinding, but the country girl who'd walked into his mom's kitchen stole his heart.

He fought the urge to walk over and pull her into his arms. Instead he made a beeline for the oversized coffee maker, filled a mug and took it to her. "Good morning."

"Same to you. Thanks." She took the mug and glanced up at him. "Aren't you having any?"

"Um… sure." Damned if she wasn't looking at him as if she liked what she saw, scruff and all. "I just—" He hadn't been this tongue-tied with a member of the opposite sex since fifth grade. But that soft flannel shirt... the way it brought out the green in her eyes....

"Just what?"

"Nothing. Never mind. Can I get you a cinnamon roll?"

"I can get it. Why don't you go pour yourself some coffee?"

"Great idea. Will do." He was acting like an idiot. Worse yet, his entire family had noticed. The looks flying around the room spoke volumes.

As he filled a mug with the rich brew his mom preferred, Clint showed up at his elbow. "I knew you were addlepated over her, but I didn't realize it was this bad."

"Hey, it's early. I'm not awake, yet."

"Nice try. You delivered her coffee so fast I thought you were on roller skates."

"Don't tease him, bro." Sky came to his rescue and handed him a cinnamon roll on a saucer. "This is new territory for our boy."

Beau took the saucer and squared his shoulders. "I'm fine. It's only that I've never had one of my girlfriends stay overnight here. It's weird."

"Come to think of it, none of us have done that." Clint lightly punched his shoulder. "My apologies, dude. I didn't think of it that way. By the time Penny was here for a sleepover, she was already a member of the family."

"Just barely." Sky glanced over at Penny, who'd joined Angie and Jess by the stove. "I felt the shift in the dynamic." He lowered his voice. "I'll bet we all did, even if we were too protective of Penny to say so. We've kept this house private for so long that bringing her in seemed…"

"Like nothing would ever be the same?" Beau picked up his roll and took a generous bite. The familiar taste grounded him some.

"That's it." Sky kept it down to a murmur. "Don't get me wrong. I was thrilled to have her here. And she fits in great. But the family had permanently changed, something that hadn't happened since… well, since Angie was born. It felt very different."

Beau chewed and swallowed. "I know what you mean. When Jess broke up with me, I was upset, but relieved, in a way. I could picture her changing things, too, and I was resisting it."

"And she has changed things, hasn't she?" Clint polished off his roll. "Could be inevitable."

"It was an *accident*, Clint."

"My point is you guys are past thirty. Cheyenne and I are nudging up against that number. Makes sense that we'd start moving in this direction."

"What direction?" Beau eyed his brother with suspicion. "If you're hinting that it's time we *settle down*—"

"Calm yourself, dude. I hate that phrase as much as you. I'll likely be raising a ruckus until the day I go toes up. But the clock's ticking. Might be I need to find a partner in crime."

Beau drained his coffee mug. "You've got us."

"Sure, but…" He grinned. "You lack some of the essential qualities I'm looking for." He tipped his head in the direction of the ladies. "If you get my drift."

"I do." Sky's gaze warmed. "And I highly recommend that route."

"That's fine for you," Beau said, "but I—"

"Ladies and gentlemen." His mom raised her voice. "That snow's not going to shovel itself. Let's get to work."

A chorus of *yes, ma'ams* was followed by everyone finishing up.

Cheyenne and Clint handled the few dishes that needed washing while Sky delegated a crew to dig their way to Buck and Marybeth's cabin another one to clear a path to the tractor barn. That would also free up the snowmobiles in case anybody absolutely had to get somewhere.

Beau took a breath. He and Jess were the only ones left without an assignment. He'd have time alone with Jess. She'd likely take the opportunity to give him her decision. Sky winked at Beau as he directed them to the horse barn path.

Maybe Jess hadn't seen that wink, but her grin as she walked with him to the entryway told him she likely had.

"I'll bet Angie told you the horse barn path was the sweetheart deal." *Sweetheart deal*? He flushed. That had come out wrong. Or right.

"She told me. Where do we get the shovels?"

"Marsh probably hauled them from the woodshed last night when he took Sam out. If so, they'll be waiting for us on the porch."

"Marsh said they're out there." Bret came up behind them, a pair of rubber boots in his hand. "Want to try these on, Jess?"

"Sure. Thanks." She took the boots, leaned against the wall and pulled them over her sock feet. "Perfect. How'd you know?"

Bret shrugged. "I can usually look at a horse's hoof and gauge the shoe size without measuring. And feet are feet, when you get down to it."

"That'll make a good comment for the article I do on you and Gil." Jess tugged her stocking cap over her bright hair and pulled up the hood on her borrowed parka for extra protection. "Let's do it."

He crammed on his Stetson, put on his gloves and turned up his collar. Then he glanced at Jess, who looked cuter than a speckled pup in her borrowed clothes. "You're with me."

"I know." There was that grin again. "Lead the way."

<u>14</u>

Jess had never seen Beau so flustered. Would the decision she'd made, the one that sent her heart racing, make him worse or calm him down? She couldn't keep that decision to herself much longer. It tumbled around in her chest, messing with her breathing and making her dizzy.

He handed her a shovel. "Let's work side-by-side for a while and see how it goes. When you get winded, stop and let me know."

"Don't worry. I've got this." The exercise would be good for her jumpy nerves. She'd tell him once they'd reached the barn and fed the animals.

He paused. "Maybe you shouldn't be shoveling."

"Why not?"

"You're pregnant. I could handle this alone."

She smiled. "I'll bet your mother shoveled while she was pregnant."

"She did, but—"

"Doc Bradley said I'm fit as a fiddle and I can do anything I feel like tackling. Let's go, cowboy." She dug the edge of her shovel into the snow and flung a decent-sized mound to one side.

He followed suit, and they worked without talking, their breath clouding the air. The shouts and laughter from the others gradually faded as the groups made progress toward the tractor barn and the Weavers' house.

The fairy lights in the trees made the snow sparkle and the dusk-to-dawn light over the barn door provided a beacon in the dark. Gradually the sky at the horizon went from pitch-black to pale gray.

Physical effort kept her warm and it also turned out to be a great distraction from her jitters. Her arms ached a little, but she pressed on, eager to get to the barn so she could give him the news. She could do this. She—

"Jess, stop." His hand gripped her arm, holding her still.

"Stop?" She glanced up at him and gulped for air. "Why?"

"You're breathing like a freight train. I asked if you wanted a break and you were breathing so loud you didn't even hear me."

"I was concentrating." Yeah, she was winded, but so what? "I was in the zone."

"Hey." He buried the blade of his shovel in the snow and took her by the shoulders. "Tell me the truth. How are you feeling?"

"My arms ache a little, but we don't have that much more. Let's keep going. The animals need food."

"How much shoveling did you do in Philadelphia?"

"None. I lived in the city and we had plows."

"And since you've been here?"

"I've cleared off the walkway to my house a few times."

"Which might be thirty feet. I believe that you're fit as a fiddle. I don't think you're in shape for sixty yards and if you end up sore because you volunteered to help today, I'll never forgive myself."

"Oh, come on. Sore muscles aren't the worst thing in the world. I want to finish the job."

"I'm taking your shovel." He closed his gloved fist around the handle.

"No, you're not." She tightened her grip.

His gaze held hers. "You know you'll lose this contest."

"Not if you're the gentleman I think you are."

"A gentleman wouldn't have given you a shovel in the first place."

"That's nonsense. Misplaced chivalry. Let go of my shovel."

"No, ma'am."

"I insist." She gave the shovel a tug. It might as well have been stuck in a block of cement.

"Jess…." He gazed at her in frustration. "Oh, hell." Nudging back his hat with his free hand, he cupped the back of her head and claimed her mouth in one swift motion.

She gasped, which allowed him to take the kiss deeper. His tongue became involved, then hers. The shovel dropped to the snow as he pulled her in as close as her parka and his shearling coat would allow.

It wasn't close enough for her. Winding her arms around his neck, she mashed her body against his and moaned as he took even more liberties with her willing mouth. The guy could kiss like nobody's business and he was employing that skill to great advantage.

The heat settling in her core added to the warmth she'd built up during the shoveling. She squeezed her hand between their bodies and began to unbutton his coat. She wanted... everything.

He lifted his mouth a fraction from hers, his voice rasping, his breathing labored. "What are you doing?"

Her fingers stilled. "Unbuttoning your coat?" It sounded crazy when she said it out loud.

"Then what?"

"Guess I'll unzip your—" She laughed, unable to finish that ridiculous sentence.

"Jess..." He dragged in a breath. "We can't—"

"I *know*, silly. But when you kiss me, I—"

"I love hearing that." He drew back and gazed at her. "Will you stay with me, then? Is that what this means?"

"I wanted to finish shoveling the path before I told you."

He pulled her in tighter, his gaze intense. "It's the right decision. You won't be sorry."

"I hope not. Now let's get this path shoveled." She retrieved hers and gave him a look. "And I *am* helping."

"Okay. But if you don't mind, I'd like to take it slow enough to have a conversation."

"About what?"

"Plans for this week." He began shoveling. "Now that I know you're staying."

"All right." She matched his more leisurely pace. "What sort of plans? Other than the obvious."

"How about taking a trail ride this weekend?"

"Sounds great."

"It would give us an hour or two to talk, find out things we don't know about each other."

"Clearly there was plenty I didn't know about you." Now that she wasn't flinging snow so energetically, she had the time to enjoy his manly display of muscular activity.

"Even though we the same year in school, we didn't hang out."

"Nope." She just ogled him on the football field.

"Weren't you editor of the school paper?"

"I was. Yearbook, too."

"Meanwhile, I was in my cool jock stage. Sickeningly full of myself."

"Yes, you were."

"Was I rude to you? I hope to hell I wasn't, but—"

"You were the sexiest guy I'd ever seen. I had a grizzly-sized crush on you."

"I had no idea."

"I admired you from afar. We moved in different circles. You probably didn't notice me at all."

"Oh, I noticed you. But since you didn't throw yourself at me, I wasn't willing to put in the effort when others were... well, you know."

"Oh, I do know. That's why I never would have asked you out. Not then and not back in November."

"Then it's a good thing I got smart and asked you." He chuckled. "Although when I walked you to your car, I half expected you to ask me."

"See? I could tell you were expecting it. No way, mister."

"And no way was I going to let you drive away without agreeing to have dinner."

"And a movie. Don't forget you offered to take me to a movie."

"Didn't make it, did we?"

"Nope."

"Still haven't."

"Because we were fixated on—"

"I'll admit it. I was."

"So was I."

"I'm just saying this coming week will be different." Snow surrendered to his blade's steady pattern of thrust and release. The guy could turn shoveling into foreplay.

She wouldn't point it out, because he was valiantly trying to change the direction of their relationship. He didn't want it to be based entirely on sex anymore, and that was a worthy goal.

Attainable? She couldn't say. He oozed pheromones, always had. She had no objection to his innate sex appeal. But when he made fun of an institution she held dear... she had a problem with that.

To his credit, he hadn't cracked a joke since they'd come out here. That might be a record.

"Sky said you bring the pigs to this barn whenever the weather's bad."

"Got to. It's in their contract. One misstep on my part and they'll have me in court."

"Come on, Beau. You're crazy about Slim and Pickens. You'd never let them suffer if you can help it."

"I like those pigs, but I'm in it for the money."

"What money?"

"I'm training them. Before you know it, they'll be an attraction. I'll put signs out on the highway and have me a pig circus bringing in big bucks."

"You are so full of it. Those races are for their benefit, because they love doing it. It's cute, but not spectacular enough to bring in spectators."

"Not yet. Just wait'll I put saddles on those pigs and train a couple of Chihuahuas to be jockeys. Now we're talking high finance."

"Why not just say you're nuts about those two animals and you'd do anything for them?"

He stopped shoveling and turned to her. His voice softened. "You're trying to make a point, aren't you?"

"Yes."

Gazing at her, he took a deep breath and let it out, creating a puff of fog. "You're right. I love those pigs something fierce. They're so damned funny and smart and affectionate, sometimes they make my throat hurt."

Now her throat did, too. "Thank you."

"I joke around about things I care about. Always have. I'll work on it."

She nodded and kept a grip on her shovel. Reaching for him would add another delay to the animals' feeding time. But oh, did she want to. That admission hadn't come easily, but he'd made it.

15

"Time to speed it up." Beau wielded the shovel with more force. "We're almost there. Let's get 'er done."

"Works for me." Jess flashed him a smile.

Did she get that he needed some time with his thoughts? If so, he was grateful.

The pig discussion had sobered him in more ways than one. She'd given him a taste of what he'd let himself in for.

She didn't just want him to stop cracking jokes all the time. She wanted him to talk about his feelings. He hadn't bargained on that.

He might have to do some fancy footwork to convince her he was good dad material without completely baring his soul. He hadn't had to bare much of it to confess the pigs were important to him. If that helped her see he'd be a loving father, so much the better.

Big surprise, he and Jess looked at things differently. Getting to know each other could mean one thing to him and something else to her. He was going for the basics — what favorite games she'd played as a kid, what music she'd listened to as a teenager, what movies she'd liked and what kind she liked now.

He'd be happy to share that type of info about himself, but there were a few topics, one in particular, he'd rather not delve into. Maybe that's why he hadn't taken her into his room while they'd dated.

Last night had been worth risking it. She'd asked about the dragon kite, like most people would. Well, if she had more questions, he'd answer them without going into detail. Come to think of it, there weren't any details to go into.

The barn was dead ahead, only a few more shovels full and they'd be done. He'd worked up a sweat during that last stretch. Could be a combination of the physical exertion and the mental gymnastics.

He was so ready to get out of his head. Feeding wouldn't take long. Nobody would expect them to come straight back. She'd agreed to stay with him and he wanted to... celebrate that fact.

A whinny came from inside the barn. Then another, followed by squeals and grunts.

She chuckled. "It's Slim and Pickens."

"Yes, ma'am. We need to get in there. Don't worry about doing a perfect job. The tractor will be over later in the day to plow the whole yard."

"Gotcha. The pigs must be close to the front since we can hear them so well."

"First stall to the right."

"Do you have food for them?"

"Yes, ma'am. It's in a couple of plastic bags in the mini-fridge in the tack room, one for each. We'll feed them first."

"Of course we will. Did you bring those guys over in the back of your truck?"

"I, um, came up with a different system."

She grinned at him. "They rode in the cab, didn't they?"

"It's really cold in the back of the truck. Slim's learned to sit in the passenger seat with a harness. Pickens curls up in a bed on the floor. They're good travelers."

"You don't have to explain it to me. I think it's adorable."

"Not sure how I feel about being called adorable. Doesn't sound particularly manly."

"How about considerate?"

"Better." He tossed one last shovelful of snow aside. "That's enough. Could you hold this while I wrestle open the door? It's likely frozen shut." He handed over the shovel and grasped the wooden bar holding the double doors shut. Took some doing, but he finally managed to slide it free.

Opening one side, he motioned her through. "Just lean those up against the wall close to the door so we don't forget 'em when we head back."

"Will do."

He pulled the door shut and latched it from the inside so it wouldn't blow open.

"Ah, nice and warm in here." She threw back her hood and pulled off her knit hat just as he flipped on the overhead lights.

Her hair glowed like fire, and he wanted his hands in it, wanted his hands on her creamy skin, too. She claimed to have had freckles when she was young, but he hadn't found more than a handful. And he'd searched.

"So many horses. I didn't know you had such a barn full."

"One for each of us. Technically Angie has two, the horse she rides and her Shetland. Although at this point Silky Boy is more of a family pet than Angie's pony."

"I see that little guy down there. Cute."

"And he knows it." The animals had quieted down when the lights came on, but now they were making noise again. "Breakfast's coming, guys and gals." Beau nudged back his hat, unbuttoned his coat and glanced at Jess. "Ready to feed some critters?"

She gazed at him, a smile tilting the corners of her kissable mouth.

"Stop looking at me that way, lady. I'm only human."

"Sorry."

"Tack room's right behind you."

"Yessir." She whirled around and pointed to an open door.

"That's it." He followed her in, keeping his hands to himself. "I'll get the bowls. I put them on a high shelf."

"So the pigs can't reach them?"

"Very funny." He gazed at the shelving that took up one wall. Bridles were stored on the opposite wall and saddles on the back wall. The tack room was crowded, but so far they hadn't had to enlarge it. "The top shelf was the only place left."

She pulled the bags of cut-up veggies out of the fridge and closed the door. "I see what you mean. Do you need all that?"

"Some of it, like the grooming totes and the cleaning supplies. Some's just there because of sentimental value. Bret made that metal boot scraper in fourth grade. Doesn't work very well, but Mom can't bear to throw it away."

"The halter next to it looks old, too."

"Yeah, that was Joker's. My first horse."

She glanced up at him. "Did he die?"

"Eight years ago. The halter's still useable, but it has his name stitched on it, and I..."

"Of course you don't want to throw it away. Or put it on another horse." She gave his arm a squeeze.

"Can't use it on someone else. You'd give that poor horse identity issues."

"Beau."

"Well, you would." He managed a smile. "Let's get those pigs fed." He held the bowls while she emptied a bag into each one. "Which one do you want to feed?"

"Pickens."

"I would've guessed that." He took the bowl with Slim's name on it and ushered her out of the tack room. "Pickens is a crowd pleaser. But Slim's smarter."

As he followed Jess to the stall with the pigs, he sucked in air. She would have to notice that halter. Now he was back in his head again.

Did he make jokes *every* time something emotional came up? Surely not. But he'd done it twice now with Jess since they'd started this barn gig, and she wasn't letting him get away with it.

Bringing her into his world for a solid week had seemed brilliant last night. He'd get a chance to prove he was worthy of taking care of their baby. He and Jess would enjoy some nice sex along the way. That program might not be as simple as he'd figured on.

<u>16</u>

Jess started laughing the moment Beau opened the stall door. Pickens, the black and white pig, wagged his tail so fast his little rump wiggled. She'd swear he smiled, too. "Here you go, Pickens." She set the bowl of chopped veggies in front of him and he went to work with a happy grunt of joy.

Slim, all black and slightly larger than Pickens, was equally excited. Beau stood back, his brown eyes sparkling with humor. "They surely enjoy life."

"That's the truth. How old are they?"

"Marsh thinks about a year and a half. He helped me rescue them from a hoarding situation he'd heard about, so we don't know for sure."

"I don't remember you mentioning you rescued them." Beau had more layers than an onion.

"Might not have. For a while I had a bunch of 'em in that pen."

"What happened to the others?"

"Adopted 'em out. Would've kept them but I couldn't do that and maintain my business."

"That story sounds tailor-made for the *Sentinel*."

"Matter of fact, your dad did cover it. The publicity helped me find folks to take them."

"That's awesome."

"Have you contacted your dad this morning? Does he need you to come in?"

"I haven't talked to him since last night. He told me then not to come in until the roads are cleared. He and Monica can handle things this morning."

"That's good. By noon the roads should be—" A loud snort from the adjoining stall made him pause. "That'll be Trigger, reminding me it's feeding time. We can leave the pigs to it. I don't know about you, but I'm ready to ditch my coat."

"Me, too."

"Just drape it over the stall door for now."

She followed his lead and left her coat behind as he secured the stall and started down the wooden aisle, closely observed by every horse in the place.

"Your horses are watching you."

He chuckled. "They know once I head for the storeroom, they're about to get their hay flakes. I'll load up a wheelbarrow and you can help me deliver them. You'll need your work gloves, though. The hay's scratchy."

"This is fun. I'm starting to feel like a cowgirl."

He gave her an appreciative glance. "You look like one in that shirt."

"Thanks. Angie said I could have it."

"Take her up on it. That girl has enough plaid flannel shirts to outfit half the town."

"I will. It's amazingly soft."

"Mm." His gaze heated. "I just bet—" He looked away and cleared his throat. "By the way, can you ride? I didn't think to ask. I assumed—"

"I can." She took a quick breath. One sizzling look and she was a befuddled mess. "I had friends with horses."

"Ever wanted one?"

"I did, but I'd have had to board. It's not the same."

"It isn't. The only disadvantage of having my own place is the distance to the barn."

"Could you have a little mini-barn out there?"

"Champion wouldn't like it. Horses feel better as part of a herd, so we keep ours here."

"Come to think of it, my friends with horses never had just one, either."

"I shouldn't complain about the distance. It's not that far." Pulling on his gloves, he took one of the wheelbarrows leaning against the back wall and rolled it toward a closed door on the right. "If you'll open it for me, you can go on in and meet Miss Kitty."

"A cat?"

"Best mouser in the county."

Jess ducked around him and opened the door. To the left of it, a glossy orange and white tabby rose from a cushy bed, stretched and padded over to meet her.

Crouching down, Jess let the cat smell her fingers. "Hello there, pretty girl."

The tabby rubbed her chin against Jess's hand and purred.

"Sounds like you got her motor running." Beau rolled the wheelbarrow over to a stack of hay flakes, put on his gloves and started loading.

"She's a sweetie. Should I close the door?"

"Not an issue. She has a cat door so she can patrol."

"I see it, now. I'll bet she loves having the run of the place."

"She does, except when Sam's in the barn. She terrorizes that poor dog. We finally installed a latch on the cat door for whenever Sam's visiting the barn."

"Aw, why do you torment that nice doggy?" Jess scratched Miss Kitty's head and gazed into her green eyes. The cat blinked as if to say *why not?*

"In her mind, Sam's trespassing." Beau chuckled as he tossed another hay flake in the wheelbarrow. "She thinks she owns the place."

"Sounds just like Midnight." Multitasking, she scratched Miss Kitty's head while checking out Beau in working cowboy mode.

She'd missed this arousing tableau while they'd dated. He'd always looked the part, but his practiced movements as he loaded the wheelbarrow created a fizzy sensation in her stomach.

"This'll take care of about half of them." He rolled the wheelbarrow over to her and hunkered down. Taking off his glove, he held out his hand to Miss Kitty.

The cat abandoned Jess immediately and went right to him. Smart kitty.

"How long has she lived here?"

"Let's see." He ran his knuckle along her chin, coaxing the loudest purr Jess had ever heard from any cat. "Marsh found her outside his apartment when he was in vet school at Rocky Mountain College. That was about ten years ago."

"Judging from how easily you made friends with Midnight, I figured you must know cats."

His amused gaze met hers. "Not well enough, apparently."

"I just realized something."

"You'll need to bring him to the cabin?"

"Bingo. My dad's feeding him this morning, but I'm not going to make him cat-sit while I'm out here. Do you have any problem with my bringing him—"

"I don't. I'm happy to include Midnight in the invitation."

"Okay, then. I'll bring his scratching post, too."

"Don't bother with cat toys. I'll just throw some condoms on the floor."

She giggled.

"Sky told me we'd eventually see the humor in it. Seems like we're there."

"Guess so."

The gleam in his eyes underwent a subtle change. "Ready for the next phase?" He stood.

Her pulse rate picked up as she got to her feet. "What's that?"

"I'm desperate to make love to you, Jess."

She gulped as a blast of adrenaline left her shaky. "I, um, expected that tonight—"

"I don't want to wait that long."

She gasped. "H-here?"

"Yes, ma'am." His chest heaved. "But you have a say in the matter. A blanket on a bed of straw might not be up to your standards."

"I..." The concept left her breathless. "I've never—"

"Okay, maybe we shouldn't—"

"There's a first time for everything." Her heart pounded.

"And I haven't shaved."

"I didn't mind it." She swallowed. "When you kissed me before, I mean." This was happening. As soon as they fed the animals, they'd...she started quivering again.

"I tried to be careful." His eyes darkened. "I'd be careful this time, too, Jess. I don't want to give you razor burn."

"I don't care." When he looked at her like that, a hormonal flood turned her knees to rubber and her insides into a carnival ride.

"I want to kiss you right now." His jaw tightened. "But...."

She held her breath, her feet stuck to the floor.

A soft meow confused her. Oh, yeah. The cat.

He glanced down. "Hey, Miss Kitty." Crouching, he stroked her from head to tail as she arched her back and purred. "Hope you'll forgive me, girl, but I'm gonna close the latch on your cat door for a little while. And this time it has nothing to do with the dog."

17

Beau was crazy about every single horse in the barn, even his mom's palomino Trigger, who was a pain in the ass. That said, he couldn't get through the feeding routine fast enough.

Jess caught on quickly and almost matched his pace delivering hay flakes to the hay nets. She was chatty, too, throwing out comments and questions as they worked. The exchanges ramped up the buzz he had going. Feeding the critters had never be this frantic. Or exciting.

"Trigger's gorgeous," she called out as she came to the palomino's stall at the end of the row.

"Don't let him hear you say that. He already admires himself something terrible."

"I think he might have heard me since I'm in his stall delivering his breakfast." She murmured something to the horse that Beau couldn't make out and Trigger snorted. "He says he'll be more modest in the future."

"He's said that before." He grabbed another hay flake from the wheelbarrow. "Then he arches his neck and prances around the pasture like he's all that and a bag of cow chips."

"Does he know your mom is a bestselling Western author?"

"I'm sure she's told him." He moved to the next stall.

"Then you can't blame him for being proud that he's carrying M.R. Morrison on his back."

"I suppose. And she did buy him a flashy saddle with jewelry on it."

"Like what?"

"Silver and semi-precious stones. It's flashy." He took the last hay flake into Buttermilk's stall. The buckskin mare was Angie's. She'd named her after Dale Evans' horse, pleasing his mom immensely.

"I'd love to see Trigger all decked out in his fancy saddle."

"That can be arranged." He dropped the flake into Buttermilk's hay net, gave the mare a friendly pat on the rump and walked out of the stall. He came face-to-face with Jess.

She was breathing fast. "Are we done?"

His body clenched in anticipation. "Yes, ma'am. Just need to put away the wheelbarrow and get a blanket." He grabbed the wooden handles and started back down the aisle, moving fast.

She kept up with him. "I figured out where you're going to put the blanket."

"Did you, now?"

"It's obvious. The stall across from the pigs is empty but there's straw on the floor."

"Yes, ma'am." Lust rose like sap in his needy body.

"Why is that?"

"Mom likes to keep a stall ready when the Wenches spend the night."

"She makes some of them sleep in the barn?"

Laughing helped tame his raging libido. "They sleep in the house. Nancy's horse stays in the barn."

"Ah, she rides over."

"She's the only one who lives close enough."

"Do you ever call her Miss Nancy?"

"Not so much anymore, but I had to work at it with all of them."

"I was still using Miss when I interviewed your mom last fall. She was very firm about dropping it, with her and all the Wenches. It's been tough to switch over, though. It's how I was taught when I was six."

"Same here. I've had years to practice and I still slip up." He leaned the wheelbarrow against the back wall and headed toward the tack room for a blanket. If he stopped moving, he was liable to grab Jess and kiss the daylights out of her.

"They're not really a book club, though, are they?" She kept up with him just fine. "I mean, in the way I think of one, where women sit around sipping wine and eating cheese and crackers."

"They do that. In summer, it's margaritas. They focus on one author instead of many, but the term still fits."

"Guess so. It was fun for me having Mom gone for the night. Dad let me stay up past my bedtime."

"We'd all camp out at Buck and Marybeth's on those nights. They taught us to play poker."

"So that's where it started."

"Oh, yeah, they're both card sharks." He ducked into the tack room. Was the blanket he wanted still there? Heart pounding, he searched the packed shelves.

"Too bad they couldn't stay last night." She'd walked in behind him.

The heat of her body called to him. He resisted the urge to turn around. He'd take this slow even if it killed him. "Unless the weather's bad, they'll stay for poker after Angie's party." There it was, soft wool with a subtle Native American design. Perfect. He pulled it down from the shelf.

"You seem to know what you're looking for."

He turned, the blanket in his arms. "I do."

"Because you've done this before?"

"Never." Wanting her this much and not acting on it made him dizzy.

"Never? Come on, Beau. Do you mean to tell me that—"

"Ridiculous, isn't it? But it never felt right, bringing a girlfriend to the barn for sex."

"Then why me?"

"Because we're not having sex."

Her brow creased. "But I thought—"

"We're going to make love." Which involved restraint on his part. Not easy. He reached for her hand and brought it to his lips, brushing them over the tips of her fingers.

"Do you think there's really a difference?"

"Yes, ma'am." He'd always used the term *having sex* because that wasn't scary. He could go for the gusto and bypass the emotional component. He was in brand-new territory and mentally crossing his fingers.

He led her out of the tack room and opened the door to the vacant stall. "Sure is bright in here. Not particularly romantic."

"Let's turn off the overhead. The sun must be up."

"No windows in here, though. We'd be fumbling around in the dark."

"Think you'll lose me?"

He dragged in air. "No, I just... wait, I know what we need. I saw them earlier." He handed her the blanket. "Be right back." He hurried into the tack room and zeroed in on Joker's halter. Yes! Two small battery-operated lanterns sat next to it.

If luck was with him, the batteries hadn't died. The first one he tried rewarded him with a soft glow. Its partner was equally cooperative. Excellent.

Lanterns in hand and a fierce ache in his groin, he flipped off the wall switch by the barn door and returned to Jess. The stall was in deep shadow until he lifted the lanterns.

And went completely still. The warm light revealed a scenario right out of his dreams — Jess lying naked on a blanket, her hair loose around her shoulders, her head propped on her hand, waiting for him.

He gulped. "Thank you."

"I decided to get this party started."

The roaring in his ears almost blocked her breathless words. "Good."

"I didn't think you'd mind."

"Mind? I couldn't be happier." *Breathe.* "Think I'll put these somewhere before I drop 'em." He hung one on each of the two hooks holding the empty hay net.

"You're right about the blanket."

"I am?" In his dazed state, he had no clue what she was talking about. He leaned against the stall and pulled off his boots, his hands unsteady.

"It's soft." She ran a hand along the material. "And thick. The straw isn't poking into me."

"Good." He tossed his boots and socks aside. Something else was growing thicker by the second and there was nothing soft about it. He'd have to peel off his jeans with care or risk an unwanted explosion.

"It's hard to believe you've never done this before. The barn is so cozy."

"Yes, ma'am." He wrenched his half-unbuttoned shirt and T-shirt over his head.

"And private. It's like we're shut away from the world."

"Unless you count the horses and a couple of pigs." Thank the Lord he'd remembered to lock up Miss Kitty.

"Will we disturb them?"

"Probably better if we don't yell." Advice for him more than her. Damn his clumsy fingers. He fumbled with his belt and finally unbuckled it.

"I won't. I didn't yell at my place. I didn't want to scare Midnight. I wouldn't want to scare those pigs. They're so sweet, and I—" She stopped talking and stared at him.

"What's wrong?" He stepped out of his jeans and briefs.

"Nothing." Her voice sounded strangled. "Could you... could you come down here, please?"

"That's my plan." He fought dizziness as he sank to his knees at the foot of the blanket.

"All the way down." She held out her arms.

"Yes, ma'am." Moving over her, he gazed into the luminous depths of her green eyes. Got lost there. "Feels like..." He paused to swallow. "Like the first time."

"I know." She quivered. "Maybe because we don't have to use anything?"

"Maybe." But that wasn't it. He was swamped with emotions that had never been a part of this. Hesitation. Tenderness. Gratitude.

"When you took off your jeans, I remembered that." She ran her hands down his back and spread her fingers over his glutes. "I knew it before, but the reality..." Her fingers flexed. "It turns me on."

"I was already turned on." He cleared the hoarseness from his throat. "Now I'm worried." Whoa, never admitted that before. "What if I—"

"We'll just do it again."

That surprised a laugh out of him, which turned into a cough.

"Easy, cowboy." She patted him on the back. "Don't hurt yourself."

He finally calmed his breathing. Sort of.

She rubbed his back. "Maybe doing it without a condom is no big deal."

"Maybe." He eased forward and... ah, hell... so good. Because he wasn't wearing a condom? Or because making love to Jess was an incredible privilege?

He closed his eyes. Forced himself to stop. If he went all the way, he'd come. He opened his eyes and gazed down at her. So beautiful.

"It's a big deal." Her rosy lips were parted, her cheeks flushed and her pupils dilated like they were when she was close. "Don't stop."

"I need to get a grip."

"Oh."

"And kiss you." Leaning down, he nibbled on her lips. "I love kissing you."

"Mm." She cupped the back of his head, pulling him closer, teasing him with her tongue.

He concentrated on the kiss, making love to her mouth without scraping her face with his beard. Slowly he gained control over his response.

She murmured something against his mouth.

"Hm?" He kissed her cheeks and her chin.

"More." Her voice was little more than a whisper. "More, please."

"Yes, ma'am." As he inched forward, every subtle ripple, every slight squeeze threatened to send him over the edge.

He pushed deeper. "Ready?"

Her gasp of agreement was followed by a soft moan.

"Come for me." He buried his cock to the hilt.

Arching upward, she clapped a hand over her mouth to muffle her cry of release.

He clenched his jaw and welcomed the force of her climax. *Intense.* Could he hold back? Yes. Worth it. So worth it.

Breathing hard, she wrapped her arms around him and held on as tremors shook her. When they finally eased, she sank back to the blanket and gazed up at him. "You didn't come."

"I wanted to be there when you did."

"Could you feel a difference?"

"*Oh*, yeah." No question. Making love won out over having sex.

"It's nice without a condom."

"That, too." The sight of her looking all rosy and contented because of what they'd shared warmed him from the inside out. If he had anything to say about it, they wouldn't be *having sex* ever again.

_18_

Jess gave this episode in the barn with Beau fifteen out of ten stars, and they weren't even done. Or were they? Although he remained firmly connected, he'd made no move to do anything about it. Instead he seemed content to stay like this and look at her.

She peered up at him. "You're not thinking you'll pull some macho ninja stunt and deprive yourself, are you?"

He smiled. "No, ma'am."

"Good, because I wouldn't be impressed. I'd consider it needless self-sacrifice."

"I'm not the self-sacrificing type."

"I didn't think so, but I didn't think you'd hold out this long, either."

"I'm waiting for you to get your second wind."

"That's very sweet, but you were teetering on the edge before. You must be going insane by now."

"I have a different mindset, now."

"You've mentioned that. And you also said you wouldn't focus on giving me multiple orgasms. Quality, not quantity."

"Two isn't so many, and this time, I'll come with you."

"That would be lovely, but personally, I'd advise you to just go for it. That climax was a doozy for me, incredibly satisfying. I might not recover for a very long time, and meanwhile, you'd—"

"I think you're recovering already."

"How do you know? You couldn't possibly know."

"Maybe not before, but without a condom I can gather a lot more info." His hips moved, seating his cock more securely. "You're quivery in there. And your nipples are asking for attention." He cupped her breast and used the brush of his thumb to prove his point.

Point made, especially as he continued his lazy caress and her body clenched again. Then slowly, with exquisite tenderness, he began to move.

With nothing to blunt the sensitivity, even the slightest friction drove her wild. His gaze locked with hers as he rocked back and forth. "You're close. I can see it in your eyes."

"Are you close, too?"

He nodded.

"And we're barely moving."

"We don't have to. We just... ah, I felt that... you're almost..."

"I can wait. You wanted to—"

"Don't wait. I'm with you." His cock pulsed. "Let go, Jess."

His low, urgent command struck a match to the wick. The flame traveled fast and she surrendered with a soft, keening cry. A powerful release gripped her just as Beau drew back and drove in deep.

His climax rocked his muscular body and his breath hissed out through his teeth. Warmth filled her core, making her a part of his release. Nice.

He rested his forehead against hers, his breathing uneven. "Spectacular."

"Uh-huh." She couldn't put words to this yet. The bond between them had strengthened, though. That much was clear.

"I want to do this again."

"Now?"

He chuckled. "Probably shouldn't. Not that I couldn't be convinced, but we need to—"

"Rejoin the rest of the world?"

"Well said." Raising up so he was resting on his forearms, he studied her, a smile crinkling the corners of his eyes. "We might need to put ourselves back together, first."

"You think?"

"Luckily it's winter and we'll arrive at the house bundled up. But... on a more personal note, we need to make use of my bandana before we get dressed."

"I suppose so. New experience, new protocol."

"I'll give you first dibs on my bandana."

"Kind of you. Where is it?"

"Back pocket of my jeans."

"I think you'll have to move to fetch it."

"Don't want to. It's warm in here."

"Would you rather have your siblings find us like this?"

"No." He slowly disengaged and stood. "Brr."

"Chilly down here, too."

He put his bandana in her hand. "I should have brought a second blanket."

"No worries. I'll make this quick. Turn your back, please."

He obliged her. "Definitely a second blanket next time. I—hang on, that's my phone. I left it in my jacket." He walked out of the stall, striding across the aisle to where their coats hung over the door to the pigs' enclosure.

His decision to answer the phone even if he was naked in this ginormous barn made her smile. She wouldn't do that. She'd get dressed and call the person back. Taking off her clothes in the privacy of this stall was as far as she was willing to go. But shyness wasn't a problem for Beau McLintock.

She'd put her underwear on by the time he came back. "Here's your bandana." She held it out. "Who was that?"

"Sky. He's driving the tractor over and he wanted to make sure we were decent."

"I hope you lied and told him we were."

"I did."

"Do you think he believed you?"

"No. That's why he called."

She grabbed her shirt and shoved her arms into the sleeves. "How fast can he get here?"

"Two minutes."

"Yikes." She moved faster, grabbing her jeans and lying back on the blanket so she could wiggle into them.

"Don't worry." He started pulling on his clothes. "The barn's locked from the inside. I told him we were just finishing up."

She got to her feet. "That's funny."

"He thought so."

"I feel like I'm back in high school and just got caught parking in the boonies."

"Did you ever?"

"Only once. Did you?"

"Many times."

"What a surprise."

"Does it bother you that my brother knows what we've been up to?"

"I guess not, but I suspect the rest of your family has figured it out, too."

"That's likely."

"Oh, well. After we announced the accidental pregnancy last night, your family will hardly be shocked that we had sex in the barn this morning."

He pulled on his boots. "Made love in the barn."

"Made love in the barn." She walked over to him and flattened her hands against his chest. "You said that part of our relationship would be different. It is."

He slid his arms around her waist. "I'm glad." Dipping his head, he brushed his lips over hers. "The tractor's coming."

A low rumble penetrated the walls of the barn. "I hear it."

He gave her another quick kiss. "I'm gonna go turn on the overhead and let Miss Kitty out before I forget. If you'd douse the lanterns and fold up the blanket, I'd appreciate it."

"Happy to." She'd switched off the lanterns and was folding the blanket when he came back. "Sky's doing a thorough job out there."

"He's probably watching the door, waiting for me to open it. He plans to leave the tractor here so Buck can put the finishing touches on the job." He tucked his shirt into the waistband of his jeans. "He'll walk back with us."

"Finishing touches? Why not take care of it all at once?"

"If he finishes, he'll have to drive the tractor back instead of walking with us."

"Ah. He *wants* to walk with us."

"Yes, ma'am. He sent us down here hoping he'd improve my chances of getting you to stay. I'm sure he's curious as hell about the outcome."

"Then you can go out there once you're dressed and tell him I'm staying. Then he can complete the job."

"I'd rather you told him."

"Okay, then I'll—"

"We might as well play it his way. Buck will be more than happy to come down and manicure the area. He loves driving that tractor. It's new."

That made her laugh. "Then by all means. I had no idea there were so many moving parts involved."

"Am I right that you'd decided before we walked down here?"

"I made the decision last night after talking with Angie."

He smiled. "She convinced you, huh? I was hoping she might put in a good word for me."

"She did." No point in bringing up the dragon kite. That was a topic for another time. "But fair warning, she's hoping for more than a week's stay."

"I believe that. She'd love having you around for longer, but—"

"She wants us to get married."

He froze. "She said that?"

"Yes."

"What did you say?"

"That it was highly unlikely."

"Hm." He glanced away.

What? Why didn't he immediately second her conclusion?

His attention swung back to her as the tractor outside began scraping away snow. The chugging and rattling sounds made him raise his voice. "I told everyone last night that a week isn't enough time for that kind of change."

Another confusing comment. Was he talking about her or himself? "I agree with you, but Angie's not giving up hope."

Once again, his gaze skittered away. "She's a romantic at heart."

"So she said." Maybe, underneath all the jokes and smiles, so was he.

<u>19</u>

Beau waited until he and Jess had their jackets on before he opened the barn door and gave Sky a tip of his hat.

His brother made one more pass with the blade, shut down the tractor and climbed out. "You two ready for some breakfast?"

"You bet." Clouds muted the light and covered the mountains, as if they were trapped inside a jar of cotton balls. "Lots of snow out here."

"Sure is. And this baby handles it great." Sky gestured toward the green tractor, bright as a new toy. "It's only fair to give Buck a turn."

"Absolutely." Beau managed not to snicker. "We'll grab the shovels and be right with you." He ducked back into the barn where Jess stood grinning, a shovel clutched in each hand.

She handed him a shovel. "You guys are hilarious."

"Be sure to admire the tractor when we go out."

"Don't worry. I picked up on his enthusiasm for it."

Flipping off the light, he ushered her out and closed up the barn.

"Hey, Sky!" Jess headed toward the tractor. "That's a mean green machine you have there!"

Beau ducked his head so Sky wouldn't see him cracking up.

"Yes, ma'am. Cuts through the snow like a knife through warm butter. And speaking of that, Marybeth's organizing the troops and breakfast will be on the table any minute."

"Yum. Let's go." Jess took the lead.

Sky fell in on her right and Beau on her left as they headed down the path recently made wider by the *mean green machine*.

Jess glanced at Sky. "Did Marybeth make those delicious cinnamon rolls?"

"That was Mom."

"Those rolls are my favorite." Beau turned up his collar and pulled on his gloves. "She's been making them ever since I can remember."

"Does she do a lot of cooking? I got the impression that Marybeth handled most of it."

"We all cook," Sky said, "But Marybeth does the bulk of it. The rolls are Mom's specialty."

"Clearly she's perfected the process." Jess cleared her throat. "Maybe she'll teach me how during the next week."

Sky shot her a quick look. "You're staying?"

"Yes, I am. I decided last night after talking with Angie."

"Huh. She didn't say a word."

"I asked her not to. I was looking for a private moment to tell Beau and you helped provide one for us. Thank you."

"You're welcome. Glad it worked out. By the way, last report I got is the road into town is almost clear and no more storms in the forecast."

"How about the ranch road out to the highway, bro?"

"I took the time to clear it before I came over here."

And by tackling that job, he'd given Beau the opportunity to make love to Jess. "Thanks."

"Welcome."

"Looks like I can take you back after breakfast, Jess."

"Sounds good. I'll drive back out after I finish at the *Sentinel* around five."

"If you need help loading the car, I can—"

"Thanks, but I can do it."

He hesitated. "I feel like I should talk with your dad today."

"That's up to you."

"I was going to, anyway, and now it seems almost required."

"For what it's worth, he seems fairly mellow about all of this."

"He does? In his shoes, I'd be spitting nails."

She gave him a look. "Which is exactly the type of thing we need to discuss this week. Someday this baby will be a teenager, and stuff will happen and you'll be spitting—"

"I didn't say it would be the ideal reaction. Just my first impulse. I can learn to check that impulse."

"Sure you can." Sky's tone was the same one he used as the family mediator. "I'm glad Jess is willing to give this a try."

"So am I. We'll have plenty of time in the evenings to get into the subject. We could even look up online parenting articles and read those together."

"There's an idea." Sky's cheek dimpled, like he was trying to hold back a chuckle.

"Your mom must be a walking encyclopedia on parenting."

Beau nodded. "For sure." Evidently Jess had missed Sky's amused reaction to the evening online research plan. Which he'd meant sincerely, damn it.

"I'd like a chance to talk with her, see what tips she can give me. I mean *us*."

"Then it's convenient you'll be here over this next weekend," Sky said. "She doesn't work weekends."

"Then she's working today?"

Sky nodded. "She wanted to be there this morning to send us off with warm cinnamon rolls in our bellies. But I guarantee after we left she made herself a quick breakfast and disappeared into her office."

"When does she quit for the day?"

"Depends on how the writing's going," Beau said. "Some days she finishes around five. But if she's not satisfied with her output, she'll take dinner into her office and keep working, unless there's something special happening."

"Like a family meeting?"

"Like that."

She dragged in a breath. "I'm still adjusting to the fact she's M.R. Morrison. Staying here every night for a week should help me get used to it. I would hate to accidentally leak info. Isn't anybody worried I might?"

"Your mother didn't." Sky gave her an encouraging smile. "She must have been around your age when she joined the Wenches."

"She was. That's freaky to think about. I didn't have a clue, ever."

"I liked Miss Mary," Sky said. "You remind me of her."

"My dad says that, too. Alrighty, then. She set the bar, so the least I can do is step up."

"You will." Beau reached for her gloved hand and squeezed it as they approached the front porch steps. "I have no doubt."

* * *

Beau took a quick shower and shaved before driving Jess back to town. She'd chosen to wait, clean up at her house, and use the time he was in the shower to call her dad and give him a run-down. He'd agreed to meet Beau for lunch at the Fluffy Buffalo.

Tapping his thumb on the steering wheel, he looked over at Jess. "How did he sound on the phone?"

"Like he always does. Interested. Supportive. Curious about how the story will play out."

"Does he want us to get married?"

"Only if we think it's a good idea."

He asked the question that had nagged him ever since she'd mentioned Angie's preference. "Do *you* want us to get married?"

"Certainly not at this point. But I inherited the curious gene from my dad. Why are you so against marriage?"

"It ties you down, narrows your options."

"That's one side of it, I guess."

"Sounds like you're on the other side."

"Of course I am. My parents had a love match. Having a supportive partner allowed them to grow, not shrink. They took great pleasure in building the *Sentinel* into a nationally respected weekly."

"Will your dad turn it over to you someday?"

"Yes, but I hope that's far in the future." She turned in her seat to gaze at him. "I didn't ask if you had clients today."

"When I checked the weather, I cancelled all three of them. Rescheduled for next week." He smiled. "Anita Verdugo wasn't happy. She has a cranky mare who's giving her fits. I've advised her to get a second horse so the mare has company, but she doesn't want to."

"So you'll keep going out there and try to train the mare even though this lady refuses to take your advice?"

"Of course. I can't abandon that horse. Next I'll suggest a goat. I think Anita might go for that idea."

"You love this business, don't you?"

He shrugged. "Pays the bills."

She gave him a raised-eyebrow glance.

"Okay, I love it. Helping horses get along with the folks who have them makes me happy."

"Where do you see it going?"

"I'd like to do clinics, eventually take my show on the road. If I build my reputation, clients might make the trip to Wagon Train. Good for me, good for the town."

"How did we date for weeks and I never found out about this?"

"It's not all that entertaining, now, is it?"

"Yes, it is. I enjoy hearing about your plans for the future."

"Why?"

"Because it shows you want to grow and change. I find that highly entertaining." She paused. "As opposed to your made-up scheme for those pigs."

"What?" He pretended to be offended. "You don't believe I'll put those pigs' names in lights?"

"Not for a minute. Although it would be cute seeing a marquee for *The Slim and Pickens Show*."

"You just wait. I'll do it."

"For Angie's birthday party?"

He laughed. "That's an awesome idea."

His good mood from that conversation lasted until he dropped her off and drove into town. No matter how many times she'd reassured him, he dreaded facing her dad.

They'd agreed to meet at the Buffalo. Usually he walked in there smiling in anticipation of a good meal delivered by a cheerful staff. A life-sized carved wooden buffalo greeted customers when they walked in.

Literally. A motion sensor hidden somewhere in the massive creature tripped when anyone came through the door. A mournful voice that sounded like a demented cow crooned *welcooome to the buuufalooo.*

Folks loved it. They'd come in, go back out to the sidewalk and come in again, just to hear that recorded message. Clint claimed the voice of the buffalo was a restaurant secret that would never be revealed.

When Rance hired on as a bartender last year, the family waited for him to let something slip. Nope. The McLintocks, even boisterous Rance, were expert secret keepers.

Rance was working today, and Beau gave him a wave before heading for a vacant table in the far corner. When the server arrived, he seriously considered ordering a beer to calm his nerves. Instead he asked for water and obsessively sipped on it as he watched the door.

He and Andy had been extremely friendly during the pig rescue. But that was then and this was now. Sweat dampened his clean yoked shirt. What was he supposed to say to the guy? *I'm sorry I accidentally got your daughter pregnant?*

Yeah, that was exactly what he should say. Not the best conversation starter in the world, but it fit the circumstances. He should have inspected those condoms before using them. No excuses.

Andy breezed in wearing a Stetson and a shearling coat. Beau had never seen the newspaper publisher ride a horse, but if he wanted to look like a cowboy, no harm in that. Beau got to his feet.

Smiling, Jess's father walked over to the table, took off his hat and held out his hand. "Good to see you, Beau."

He gripped the guy's hand. "Mr. Hartmann, I'm so sorry that I—"

"Hey, it's Andy, son." His handshake was firm. "No apologies necessary."

"But it was my—"

"And her cat. When something that bizarre happens, I always figure the universe is having a little joke on our behalf."

"Yes, sir." He waited until Jess's dad sat before he resumed his seat.

"I think we each need a beer." Andy picked up the menu. "And a Reuben with extra sauerkraut. How's that sound to you?"

"Perfect."

"I can tell you're nervous, but you have nothing to be nervous about. You and Jess will have a wonderful baby. I mean, look at the two of you. She's beautiful and you're handsome. Come August, I'll have the prettiest grandbaby in town." He glanced up as a server arrived. 'Two lagers and two Reubens with extra kraut. Put it on my tab, please."

"Yes, Mr. Hartmann."

"Andy, I'm paying for this."

"Who says? Give up that hair shirt you're wearing, Beau McLintock. It doesn't suit you."

"And you're okay with Jess living out at the ranch for the next week?"

"Why not? The better you two become acquainted, the more likely you'll be a good team for raising that baby." Andy shrugged out of his coat and left it to hang on the back of his chair. "Look, son, I know your heart, maybe better than she does. I watched you struggle to save those pigs. You won me over then. My positive opinion about your character hasn't changed."

Beau gulped. "Thank you, sir."

"That said, Jessica is the most important person in the world to me. Cause her grief, and I'll hunt you down."

"Yes, sir. Understood." Although Jess had claimed her dad was mellow, when it came to his daughter's welfare, the gloves came off. Beau respected the hell out of that.

20

Jess worked half-a-day at the *Sentinel* and checked in with her dad before she left. It was the first chance she'd had to talk with him since he'd had lunch with Beau. "How did it go?"

"Well." He pushed his glasses to the top of his head. "He promised to take good care of you and I promised if he didn't I'd come after him."

"You didn't say that."

"Oh, yes, I did. I like the guy a lot. But that doesn't mean he has carte blanche to mess with you. And now Beau and I understand each other."

"I'm flabbergasted, Dad! I've never heard you talk like that."

"I've never had to. The guys you've been interested in have been mere blips on the radar. Beau is a major bogey, coming in hot."

"You're serious, aren't you?"

"You bet. Since your mother's not here, it's all up to me, and like I said, I never worried about the non-entities in your life prior to this. They didn't have enough substance to warrant my attention. This one does."

"Then how come you didn't say so when I was dating him in December?"

"I was working up to it. I could tell you were getting in deeper by the minute. But when I was just about to ask a few questions, you broke up with him. I let it go."

"But... when I told you about the baby, you were all happy. You even stood up for Beau, saying his jokes were a defense mechanism. Which they so are, by the way, and—"

"I am happy about the baby. Overjoyed about my grandchild-to-be. As for Beau, he has many great qualities. He's kind, generous and ethical. But he isn't keen on marriage."

"That's putting it mildly. I don't see that happening."

"Probably not, but I sensed he was feeling some pressure to *do the right thing*. Don't know where it's coming from. Desiree would never push him, but maybe his brothers, or even his little sis want him to step up."

"I can't say for sure about his brothers, but Angie definitely wants that. She's young and hopelessly romantic. But he wouldn't get married to please her."

"Or to please you?"

"Dad! I would never try to guilt him into it."

"I know you wouldn't, sweetheart. The thing is, he knows it's your dream, even if it isn't his. And he's in love with you."

Her breath caught. "He told you that?"

"He didn't have to. It was written all over his face when he talked about you. Is this a surprise? You're acting like you don't—"

"He's never said it." She paused to take in air. "For that matter, neither have I."

Her father gave her a look filled with understanding... and sympathy. "And you're in love with him, too."

"I've tried not to be."

"Aww, honey." He gathered her into a hug. "That's tough duty. Maybe this week out at Rowdy Ranch isn't such a good idea, after all." He stepped back. "You're allowed to change your mind, y'know."

"I know." She swiped at her eyes. "But everyone's expecting me. I'm scheduled to interview Bret and Gil about their metal art in the morning." She pulled a tissue out of her pocket and blew nose. "Sorry. I've been more emotional lately."

"Your mom was, too. She said it was a side effect of being preggers."

"Could be." She sighed. "I've always wanted what you and Mom had, and then I go and get knocked up by the wrong guy."

"He sincerely wants to be a good dad."

"It would be great if he can pull that off. He has some inner demons, though." She glanced at the antique Register clock on the wall. She could change her mind about spending this week with Beau, but she'd have to do it fast.

She met her dad's concerned gaze. "Going out to Rowdy Ranch is important. I've already learned more about Beau and his family in the past twenty-four hours than in the entire time we dated. The more I know, the better I can navigate through this."

"That's my girl. Knowledge is power."

"Exactly." She gave him a quick kiss on the cheek. "I'll be in tomorrow as soon as I finish the interview." She picked up her trusty camera and tucked it into her satchel. "It'll make a good feature."

"Take some pictures of those pigs while you're at it and we can run an update. The McLintocks have always been good for interesting copy."

You don't know the half of it. "I will, Dad." Maybe someday she'd try to convince Desiree to let him in on the secret. After all, he was the grandfather of this baby. That should qualify him as family, too.

* * *

Good thing she could find Beau's cabin in the dark. Cheerful lights shining from the windows brought a sigh of pleasure as she rounded the curve.

Clearly Beau had been watching for her. He walked out the door the moment she came in sight. He'd pulled on his coat but hadn't bothered to button it. Slapping his hat on his head, he crossed the porch in two strides.

He'd swept all the snow off the porch and shoveled the parking spot she'd always used, a place right next to his truck. A familiar rush of anticipation gripped her as she pulled into that spot. The security light that illuminated the parking area came on.

A night in this cabin with Beau used to be the highlight of her week. He'd never asked her to stay through a weekend and she'd never suggested it. She'd never asked him to stay at her place for the weekend, either. Hadn't dared. Her reluctance to ask should have told her something.

Midnight's non-stop yowling protest at being trapped in the carrier ended when she turned off the motor. As she unsnapped her seatbelt, Beau opened her door.

"Glad you're here. I wondered if..." He left the sentence unfinished.

She glanced up at him. "Full disclosure, I considered canceling."

Hurt flashed in his eyes for an instant. He replaced it with a casual smile and nudged back his hat with his thumb. "It's not like you signed a contract. Why don't we take it one night at a time?" He held out his hand.

"Sounds like a plan." She took his hand and...game over. His warm grip sent a current through her needy body, lighting her up from the inside out. She met the heat in his dark gaze and her breath caught.

With a soft groan, he reached in, hauled her from her seat and crushed her against his chest. His mouth found hers and his tongue thrust deep.

Hungry for the taste of him, she kissed him back as if they'd been separated for days instead of hours. She couldn't get close enough. Sliding her hands inside his open jacket, she wrapped her arms around his solid, aroused body.

With a soft groan, he reached for the top button on her coat and worked his way down. Pushing the coat aside, he cupped her breast through the soft fabric of her shirt.

Easing back on the kiss, he nibbled on her lips, his breathing and hers surrounding them in a misty fog. "You feel so good."

"You, too." She shoved her hands in the back pockets of his jeans.

"That's my cue." His voice roughened. "Let's get inside before I start undressing you right—"

A plaintive meow brought his head up with a soft curse. "I can't believe I forgot Midnight. And here I wanted to get on his good side."

"Don't feel bad. I forgot him, too. I'll go fetch him." She extricated herself from the delicious warmth of his arms and started around the back of the SUV.

"If you'll take him in, I'll unload the rest of your stuff."

"Don't be silly. I'll—"

"I'm not being silly. I'm being gallant. Like my mother taught me."

"Alrighty, then. Thank you."

"What am I looking for?"

"My suitcase is in the back seat, a satchel is on the floor in the front and all Midnight's things are in the cargo area." She opened the front passenger door and lifted out his carrier. "Hey, kitty, I'm so sorry for leaving you in the car with the door open and a cold wind blowing in."

The cat's response, a low noise in the back of his throat, told her exactly what he thought of that.

"My fault, Midnight." Beau lifted the tailgate. "I'll make it up to you. I'll bring all your belongings in first. How's that?"

"I'm sure he'll appreciate it."

"I built a fire. Maybe he'll want to curl up near it."

"We'll see. He's never had that option." She did her best to hold the carrier level as Midnight shifted around inside it and made little sounds of kitty distress.

"You'll be out of there soon, sweetheart." She carried him up the steps, through the front door and into the house.

Flames danced and crackled in the stone fireplace that anchored the wall between the living room and the kitchen. A two-sided firebox allowed it to be enjoyed from either room.

The cedar scent of burning wood, blended with a delicious aroma coming from the kitchen, brought a sigh of pleasure. Had Beau's cabin always been this welcoming?

She set Midnight's carrier on the braided rug in front of the fireplace, knelt in front of it and opened the wire door. "Welcome to Beau's house, kitty."

The cat crept out slowly, belly low, eyes wide.

"You'll like it here, I promise." Jess took a more thorough look around. The room was more pulled together than it had been in December. A couple of colorful pillows brightened the sofa and a framed print above the fireplace added a cozy touch.

The scene of a cabin in the woods at twilight, light spilling from the windows and smoke rising from the chimney, could almost be Beau's place. A fancy metal log holder stood on the hearth where the old cardboard box used to be. Bret and Gil's work?

Midnight wandered over to something in the shadows on the far side of the hearth. Standing, she walked over to see what it was. A cat bed? The plush red cover would nicely showcase a black cat. Beau must have bought it today after lunch with her dad, and...wait.... She leaned down for a closer look.

"Do you think he'll like it?" Beau came through the door with the carpeted scratching post over one shoulder and a large canvas shopping bag over the other.

"I sure hope so, since you had his name stitched on it."

"It's my way of kissing up to your cat."

"He can't read."

"Says you." He put the four-foot-tall combo perch and scratching post near the plush bed. Midnight walked straight over to the mostly shredded post and began sharpening his claws. "Good kitty." Beau nodded in approval. "Jess, what about feeding him? I see you brought his food, but I could also give him—"

"He had dinner before we left. He's fine."

"Okay, then. Hey, Midnight, what do you think of that cushy bed?"

Midnight stared up at him, tail twitching.

Beau stared back. "It has your name on it. That's how you can tell it's yours. Why not try it out?"

Turning away from the scratching post, the cat wandered over to the bed, sniffed it for a few seconds and stepped over the rolled edge. Some kneading followed, along with a gentle purr before he curled up in the cat-sized depression in the middle.

"I'll be darned." Jess glanced at Beau. "It's a hit. Thank you."

"He saw his name. That did the trick."

"Come on. He likes the bed. It has nothing to do with his name being on it."

"You can have your theory and I've got mine." He watched Midnight tuck deeper into the bed and close his eyes. "Those pigs have their names on the bowls. It matters."

"Are they bedded down for the night?"

"Yes. They said to tell you hello."

"I'm sure they did." His quirky behavior with animals had charmed her when they'd dated. It likely would charm a child, too. He'd be an entertaining dad, no question.

"Anyway, I just realized I shot myself in the foot."

"You did?"

"I set up this folksy situation with dinner simmering on the stove and a fire going, but—"

"It's lovely. What a nice welcome."

"But it's restrictive. I could turn off the heat under dinner but I can't leave the fire, especially with Midnight sleeping nearby. That means we can't—"

"That's okay with me."

"You sure?"

"Absolutely sure. Dinner smells delicious and I'm hungry as a bear."

"Great." He set down the canvas bag loaded with Midnight's essentials. "I'll bring in the rest and then we can eat."

"Sounds perfect." As he hurried out the door, she took off her coat and hung it in the hall closet. His brown canvas duster for riding in bad weather was in there, along with the sorry pair of boots he couldn't make himself get rid of. Both items were achingly familiar.

So was the constant hum of sensual tension. Lovely setting. Irresistible man. She was strongly tempted to push the issues aside and sink into the warmth of Beau's magnetic presence.

Been there. Done that. Big mistake.

21

When Jess asked for a second bowl of his chicken soup, Beau was so happy he wanted to grab her and make love to her on the kitchen table. But he didn't dare with Midnight sleeping on the other side of that firebox. He didn't want to risk freaking the cat out his first night here.

The cat served as a constant reminder of how life had changed and would continue to do so. He'd intentionally put Midnight's new bed in a spot that ruled out making love to Jess on the braided hearth rug tonight. This week was about acting like a grownup.

Putting a check on his libido, he coaxed Jess to talk about the newspaper she'd published at age eight. She'd roped in two neighborhood kids and had convinced her parents to let her use the creaky old printer they'd planned to recycle.

"I was the editor, of course." She took another spoonful of the steaming soup and held it over her bowl to let it cool. "Tommy was the distributor since he was the fastest bike rider among us. Sue was the investigative reporter, although I helped with that. We called it the *Beale*

Street Bugle, since that's the street we all lived on." She tucked the spoon into her mouth.

"Did you keep any copies?'

Nodding, she swallowed. "They're probably still in a trunk in my old room at Dad's. I should look, because some of the stories would be hysterical to read, now."

"Can you remember any?"

"Oh, yeah. There was the time Sue and I hid in the bushes for hours investigating why a red Corvette was parked in front of Mrs. Kimball's house every Wednesday between noon and three that summer. And Mrs. Kimball's drapes were always drawn during that time."

Beau grinned.

"You get it, now, but we were only eight. Totally innocent, working to solve a neighborhood mystery."

"Did you?"

"Of course! Nobody's more persistent than an eight-year-old girl except two eight-year-old girls. We scored an interview with the young guy who drove the Corvette. He told us Mrs. Kimball had a recurring plumbing issue, so that's how we wrote it up in the next issue of the *Bugle*."

"I'll bet that caused a ruckus."

Her green eyes sparkled. "After the *Bugle* hit everyone's front porch, we heard some yelling from the Kimballs' house. We decided the plumbing issue must have finally been corrected, because we never saw that red Corvette again."

He laughed. "Jessica Hartmann, girl reporter, keeping the neighborhood informed and honest."

"Which reminds me." She picked up her spoon and held it toward him as if it were a mic. "Inquiring minds want to know. Beau McLintock, did you make this fabulous soup?"

"I did."

"Did you fix it all by yourself or did you have help?"

"Marybeth coached me through the process this afternoon. But I wrote everything down. I can do it again."

"Well, this reporter gives the soup a two-thumbs up. Care to share the recipe with our viewers?"

"That might not be in my best interests."

"Why not? It could go viral."

"I'm not looking for fame and fortune, so no, thanks."

"Then perhaps Marybeth would like some publicity. It's very good soup. She could become an online sensation."

"I doubt she'll give you the recipe."

"Why wouldn't she? It's just a soup recipe."

"It's way more than that. I asked her what I could serve that would create an atmosphere of trust. She recommended her special chicken soup."

Jess narrowed her eyes. "You're making this up."

"No, ma'am. Once she said it, I knew that was the right answer. We've been eating it at Rowdy Ranch for years. The babies only get the broth at first, but the rest of us chow down on the full-bodied version. Consequently, you won't find a family more trusting than ours."

"I agree you're a close bunch, but to give the credit to this soup is—"

"Not *all* the credit. But Marybeth reminded me that whenever we've had a family crisis, whether it's sickness or something else, she makes this soup. Just the smell of it calms everyone. Reminds us we're on the same team."

Jess put down the spoon, confusion in her gaze. "Then why didn't she serve it last night?"

"I asked her that. Evidently she talked to Mom and asked if last night's family meeting was a chicken soup situation. Mom said it was a cause for celebration."

"Are you saying last night didn't rate chicken soup but tonight does?"

"Yes, ma'am."

"Why?"

"Because you don't trust me to be on your team. That's what this week is about."

"I trust you to make chicken soup."

Not much, but he'd take it. "Excellent. Babies can have the plain broth when they're around six months. Marybeth told me that, too."

"You're planning to make it for our baby?"

"I am."

"Huh."

"You look baffled."

"I just never pictured... I mean, if you're making baby food, you and I would have to coordinate that. Have a plan. A schedule."

"That wouldn't work for you?"

"For me? Sure. But I figured you'd rather interact with him or her on the fly, whenever you took the notion."

He frowned. "What gave you that idea?"

"Your objection to being tied down."

"Ah." He had said that, hadn't he? "I don't have that objection when it comes to our baby."

"Why not?"

He held her gaze while he scrambled for an answer that wasn't a joke. A real answer. "You ask tough questions."

Her intensity faded and was replaced by a soft smile. "It's what I do."

Leaning back in his chair, he shifted his attention to the fire. Just coals, now. Should he build it up again? Might depend on how this discussion went.

When he had the freedom/hogtied question sorted, he turned back to her. "I hope this isn't insulting, but the pregnancy hit me the same way as the dire circumstances of the pigs."

"I beg your pardon?" She looked a little insulted.

"Bear with me." He soldiered on. "I wouldn't have adopted a couple of pigs on my own. I wasn't looking for an extra responsibility. But then Marsh found out about the hoarding situation. I happened to be around when he was describing it to Mom. And boom, I was committed."

Her eyes widened. "Are you saying you wish I hadn't told you about—"

"No! Hell, no. Did you ever consider *not* telling me?" His gut clenched.

"Never."

Relief loosened the knot in his stomach. "Thank God. That would have been... unthinkable."

"I agree."

"Thank you for that. You could have left town without saying anything, like my mom did when she was pregnant with Sky."

"She had a reason that made sense to her. I didn't."

"Except you're not thrilled I'm the father."

"I'm not horrified, either, Beau. Please don't think that. I just—"

"I promise I'll do right by our kid."

"Out of a sense of obligation? Because that's no good."

"Obligation plays no part in it. Or duty. I just want to be… a real dad." He glanced at her. Did she get it? Was he making sense?

The warmth in her green eyes was a good sign. She reached across the table and laced her fingers through his. "And real dads make a kick-ass bowl of chicken soup?"

"Damn straight." He tightened the connection. "I have dessert in the fridge."

"I'd love to have some… later."

"Later?" That sexy murmur had promise. "How much later?"

She gave him a teasing smile. "Twenty minutes?"

"You sadly underestimate me, dear lady." He pushed back his chair and stood. "Wait here for a minute, please."

"Why?"

Leaning down, he gave her a quick kiss. "If I told you, it wouldn't be a surprise."

22

Jess wasn't the type to sit quietly and do nothing, so she gathered their dishes and carried them to the sink. She'd just started loading the dishwasher when Beau's voice, pitched low, drifted through the firebox opening. Clearly he wasn't talking to her, which left... Midnight.

Closing the dishwasher, she walked into the living room.

Her wide-awake kitty stood in the middle of his new bed, purring up a storm. Beau crouched beside him, stroking his glossy fur. He continued the caress as he glanced over his shoulder. "Found him in the middle of our bed."

"Color me shocked." *Our* bed? Since when had she acquired joint ownership?

"Guess I should have closed the door after I took your suitcase in there." He turned back to the cat and scratched along his chin, which ramped up the purr several decibels. "I forgot that's what you used to do when I came over."

"Except for the first time."

"Yeah." He chuckled. "I didn't really expect you'd invite me in that night."

"Then why did you have condoms?"

"Because it's better to be prepared and not need one than to be unprepared and miss a golden opportunity."

She grimaced. "Maybe not so golden, after all."

"Oh, yeah, it was pure gold." He kept petting the cat. "What if I'd gone my whole life convinced I didn't want a kid? As it turns out, I'm stoked about it."

"No kidding?"

"Scout's honor."

"You were a Boy Scout?"

"Well, not exactly. But Sky was and we were always wrestling. Some of his honor rubbed off on me." He looked back at her. "I've been negotiating with Midnight, hoping to convince him to curl up and go back to sleep."

"Ah."

"That's not gonna happen, is it?"

"Nope."

"Now what?"

"Did you handle whatever the surprise was?"

"I did not. When I found him on the bed, I picked him up and brought him in here. I promised him a year's supply of catnip if he'll stay in his own bed, but he's not so inclined."

"Too bad for you, he doesn't like catnip. Also, I just realized you only have two interior doors in this cabin."

"Designed it that way. Just put doors on the hall closet and the bedroom. And I'm not shutting Midnight in the closet."

"You'd regret it. He hates being closed into small spaces."

"So do I, thus the absence of doors."

"Would you mind if I give him some chicken broth?"

"No, ma'am. I'd grill him a steak if that would do the trick."

"It might, but this'll be quicker. I'll put some of his food in his bowl and add a spoonful of chicken broth. That should keep him busy for a while."

"How much time would that give us?"

"Maybe three or four minutes."

"Three or four *minutes*? I'm good, but not that good."

"I'm not buying enough time to do the deed. Only enough to dash into the bedroom and close the door."

"Oh. Then by all means, go for it."

"Once he hears me tapping a spoon on his bowl, he'll come running. And you need to—"

"Make tracks for the bedroom, close the door and set up the surprise."

"You won't have time. Leave the door open. I'll be right behind you."

"Which sucks the romance right out of this plan."

"Who says? I think working together to outwit the cat is extremely romantic. Keep petting him while I duck into the kitchen." She left quickly. She loved her cat, but she wasn't about to let him interrupt whatever romantic surprise Beau had created.

After dishing food into Midnight's ceramic bowl, a generic one without his name on it, she tapped the spoon on the edge and he came running.

She set it down on the mat she'd brought to protect Beau's gorgeous hardwood floor, left the spoon in the sink and sidled out of the kitchen. Midnight didn't even look up.

She kicked off her loafers in the living room and ran toward the open bedroom door in her sock feet. Flickering light spilled into the hall. Dashing inside, she was dazzled by a blizzard of twinkling fairy lights.

Before she could take it all in, Beau's strong arms came around her and his lips found hers. With a sigh of surrender, she melted against his muscled body. His sure hands divested her of her clothes in no time.

Scooping her into his arms, he carried her to the bed and laid her on the soft sheets lit by starlight draped across the headboard and footboard.

"This is beautiful."

"This is pretty." He kept his gaze on her as he stripped off his clothes. "You're beautiful."

"I love the fairy lights." *I love you.*

"I know. That's why I brought some inside so you could watch them sparkle while I'm deep inside you, making you come."

"You're beautiful, too." She took in the whole of him, hungry for the press of his body, the slide of his unfettered cock. Sitting up, she reached out and grasped the length of it as he neared the bed.

His breath hitched. "Go easy. I don't want to—"

"You used to like this." She sat on the edge of the mattress and drew him closer.

"I used to have more control."

"Why?" She squeezed gently, relishing the way his breathing changed.

"Don't know." He gasped as she kissed the sensitive tip and swiped once with her tongue. "You drove me wild before, but now... I..." He groaned. "Jess."

"Let me." She took him into her mouth, not all the way, but enough to make him shudder. He wasn't kidding about being more responsive. Even gentle suction made him gasp. The slightest movement of her tongue caused him to tense and swear under his breath.

"Stop." His command rang with desperation. "Please. I need... I need..."

She eased back and resisted the urge to give him one more intimate kiss. "I know what you need. So do I." She stretched out on the bed, her invitation plain. "Come on down, cowboy."

He didn't waste time. In seconds he'd moved between her thighs and claimed his reward with a force that lifted her off the mattress.

A faint meow penetrated the solid wood of the bedroom door. Then Beau drew back and thrust deep again... and again... until nothing registered but the rapid, liquid vibration as their bodies came together, the rasp of their breathing, the soft cries and drawn-out moans.

Then he slowed the pace and paused, gulping for air. "Forgive me. I got... carried away. I meant to—"

"Don't stop." Squeezing her eyes shut, she dug her fingertips into his tight buns. "Please don't stop."

"I just... open your eyes."

Dragging in a breath, her body poised on the brink of an orgasm, she looked up at him.

His dark gaze burned with fierce intensity. "I love you."

She gasped.

"I have no right to love you. I just do."

"Beau—"

"I don't expect you to love me back." He began moving again, creating delicious shock waves with every firm stroke. "I'm the wrong guy."

"But I—"

"It's okay, Jess. It's okay." He ramped up the action.

And she lost her mind. The power surge of her release lit every ecstatic nerve in her grateful body. She cried out as pleasure rolled through her, Beau's thrusts adding to a never-ending flood of sensation.

Then he pushed home one last time. With a roar of triumph, he let go, the waves of his climax melding with hers. She tightened her grip on his sweaty back and closed her eyes. He might be the wrong man. But not tonight.

23

Beau overslept. He never overslept. Prided himself on it. Disoriented, he sat up. Pale sunlight came through the window and the cabin was quiet. "Jess?" No answer. An engine revved outside.

Tossing back the covers, he stood and hurried out of the bedroom, fighting low-grade panic. Had his *I love you* scared her into packing up and leaving? Maybe he could still catch her.

He lengthened his stride, made it to the front door and opened it as her SUV pulled away. "Jess!" She kept going. He had one foot out the door when an icy wind reminded him he was naked.

Had it been summer, he would have run after her anyway. If he tried it this morning, though, he might end up with frostbite on some parts he couldn't afford to lose.

What an idiot he'd been to tell her. He was famous for opening his mouth when he should keep it shut, but this time he'd totally mucked it up. With a sigh, he closed the door, turned around and blinked.

Had she been so upset she'd forgotten to take Midnight? The cat lay curled up in his bed, his green eyes half-closed in disapproval. No telling if he objected to the recent blast of cold air or Beau's state of undress. Likely both.

Okay, dude, get a grip. He scrubbed a hand over his face. She wouldn't race off and leave her cat. He glanced at the living room clock. Geez, it was late. *And she had an interview with Gil and Bret, dumbass.*

On top of that, he had an appointment with Kendall Abbott this morning in…yikes, thirty-seven minutes. Why hadn't Jess given him a shake before she left?

Well, because he hadn't bothered to mention said appointment, had he? It was on the calendar in his phone but nowhere else. If he took a fast shower and fed the pigs instead of eating breakfast, he'd make it. Time to get moving.

Throwing on clothes out of the hamper, he quickly chopped veggies, fetched his jacket and hat from the closet and headed out back. Luckily Slim and Pickens weren't the type to hold a grudge because breakfast was a bit late.

He gave them each a quick scratch and dashed back inside. He'd just stepped out of the shower when his phone pinged with a text. He grabbed it from the bathroom counter. A text from Jess.

Are you OK? Bret thinks I should make sure you're alive. I told him you were breathing when I left. Did you get my note?

He sent a reply. *I'm fine. Hurrying to make a client appointment. See you for dinner.*

Her reply was immediate. *C U then.*

He wanted to crawl through the phone and kiss her. The scent of her shampoo teased him, as if she might appear any second. She'd never brought stuff like that before, but now it was all here — her brush and hair dryer, lotion, and some other bottles and jars from her bathroom at home.

Surprise, he liked having it here taking up space in his bathroom. Too bad he'd slept through her morning routine. He wouldn't tomorrow. If he had to set an alarm, so be it. His shower was roomy. They could—

Client appointment. Focus. He dressed quickly. She'd said something about a note. It wasn't in the bedroom, so probably in the kitchen. Glancing at the time on his phone, he quickened his step. Midnight's eyes were closed and he'd rolled to his back. Clearly he was settling in.

Jess's note lay on the cleared kitchen table. She had good handwriting, something else he wouldn't have discovered in dating mode. They'd communicated by phone and text.

Good morning, Beau,

I fed Midnight so he's good for the day. I ate a little of the cereal I found in the cupboard. We should talk about how we'll handle food expenses this week. I don't intend to freeload.

Sorry I conked out on you last night. Guess I was more tired than I thought. You must have been tired, too, since you're still out. Last night was lovely. Thank you.

Jess

He re-read the last part. Evidently his confession hadn't horrified her. She still liked him enough to thank him. But for what, exactly? Homemade chicken soup? Fairy lights? Sexual satisfaction?

Thanking him wasn't a bad thing. It just wasn't...what he wanted. He folded the note, tucked it in the pocket of his Wranglers and put on his jacket and hat.

What did he want, then? He left the cabin and coaxed his cold-sensitive truck to start. The familiar road to Kendall's neighboring ranch didn't require much attention, leaving room for the note that burned a hole in his pocket.

Nothing wrong with that note. It was polite. So damned *polite.* The muscles in his neck tightened. He rolled his shoulders a few times.

Okay, he'd invited her to stay so he could demonstrate his parental potential. The soup had been a good step in that direction. He was making progress on that front. He should be happy about that.

Hell, he should be shickled titless about everything. She'd agreed to this week-long program and was willing to make love with him while she was here. Not just willing, but eager.

Had he secretly wanted her to fall for him in the process? Last night's epic event had left them too zonked for pillow talk, but had he hoped for at least an X and O at the end of her note this morning?

Shame on him if he had. Since he wasn't convinced he could be the type of guy she was looking for, he shouldn't want her to fall for him. That made his spontaneous confession an especially bone-headed move.

What now? He couldn't exactly take it back.

Kendall met him at the round pen as usual. She'd already mounted up and was working

Mischief, the three-year-old she'd spoiled rotten from the moment he'd been born.

Beau couldn't blame her. Mischief's birth had come only days after Kendall had lost her widowed father to lung cancer. Then she'd let almost two years pass before admitting she'd created a problem.

"Morning, Beau!" She waved a greeting as he left the truck and walked toward the round pen.

He tipped his hat. "Morning, Miss Kendall!" Every time he saw her, he had to remind himself that she was a grown woman who was doing a fine job of running her dad's small ranch all by herself.

But she looked like a teenager, short and slight, with a smattering of freckles on her turned-up nose. It didn't help that she hated wearing makeup and never dressed up. She stuck with jeans and flannel shirts in winter, T-shirts and cut-offs in summer.

He took his seat on the top rail and observed for a few minutes as she put Mischief through the series of exercises he'd recommended. "Looking good, Kendall."

"He's coming around."

"He sure is. I think I've worked myself out of a job."

"I think so, too." She trotted over to where he sat and pulled Mischief to a stop. "I'm glad, but sort of sad at the same time. The lessons have been fun."

"For me, too. But now you and Angie can take that trail ride you guys talked about for his coming out party. He should do fine."

"Yep. I'll text her today. That reminds me of something else. She's finished the rewiring job in my kitchen. I'd like to get Cheyenne out here to double-check that it's no longer a fire hazard."

"Good idea." Beau managed to keep a straight face. Kendall had a huge crush on his brother, which had become obvious during his recent fire safety inspection of her house.

But she had several counts against her. She was Angie's close friend, for one thing. And although she was a year older than their little sis, she looked younger. Cheyenne was nearing thirty and said he wasn't about to start robbing the cradle.

"Do you know whether Cheyenne's at the station today?"

"I think he is, but if he's tied up, the dispatcher can always send—"

"I can wait until he's free. He's the logical one since he knows what the issue was."

"Well, there's that." He coughed into his fist to hide a chuckle. "Listen, unless you want to ride around the corral for another forty-five minutes for the heck of it, whatcha say we wrap this up and save you some money? I won't charge you for this one."

"We can end the lesson, but I'm still paying you." She dug in her coat pocket and handed him cash, her preferred method. "You blocked out this time for me. My dad used to say that time is the most valuable thing we have."

The slight catch in her voice convinced him to take the money and not argue about it. "Thank you."

"Besides, you'll be needing it, now."

"I will?"

The sparkle returned to her eyes. "For the baby."

"Oh."

She smiled. "Maybe I wasn't supposed to know about that, but—"

"Are you kidding? By now you'd be hard-pressed to find a single person in Wagon Train who doesn't know about it. I'm looking for it to be the headline in the *Sentinel* this weekend."

24

Jess had sent a text to Beau early in the afternoon that unless he had something planned, she'd bring burgers from the Fluffy Buffalo. They'd done take-out from the Buffalo several times while they were dating, so she knew what he liked on his burger. Beau had responded with *Great idea!* so she'd placed the order.

With the burgers carefully wrapped in foil and tucked into the insulated carryall she'd used back in December, she made it to his cabin as twilight descended. Lights glowed from the windows and smoke drifted from the chimney.

Home. The word lodged in her chest, bittersweet. This wasn't home and probably never would be, but darned if it didn't look like she'd always pictured the one she'd have some day.

He'd said he loved her, but that didn't change anything. Loving her didn't mean he wanted to get married and create the cozy family she dreamed of. She would have revealed her feelings last night, too, but he'd stopped her.

That was just as well. Admitting she loved him back would only add stress to an already complicated situation. Better to leave those words unsaid.

Once again, Beau came out on the porch and started down the steps as she pulled into her spot. His appearance brought a surge of pleasure that left her breathless. She was much too glad to see this cowboy.

She scrambled out before he could reach her since he was minus his hat and coat this time. "The insulated bag's behind my seat." That was a routine they'd worked out when they were dating because it was more efficient.

"Figured." Quickly opening the back door, he picked up the carryall. "Thanks for bringing dinner." Wrapping an arm around her shoulders, he started toward the steps.

"You're welcome."

"Bret and Gil are excited about that interview."

"So am I." She climbed the steps and he matched his stride to hers. They'd perfected that trick when they were dating, too. "It turned out well. The pictures are great. I can't wait for them to see it on Saturday."

"It was nice of you to do them a favor."

"I didn't do it as a favor. Or because I'm now considered a member of the family. Their metalwork is top-notch, and their story is exactly the sort of thing the *Sentinel* is designed to—"

"I think I just got my wrist slapped." He ushered her through the front door.

She groaned. "Sorry. I shouldn't have jumped down your throat. Journalistic integrity is a hot button for me."

"I should have known." He sighed dramatically as he put down the insulated bag and helped her off with her green coat. "Guess I'll have to ditch my plan to bribe you into putting those pigs on the front page."

She had to admire how fast he could lighten the mood. "Bribe me with what?"

"Doesn't matter if you're bribe-proof." He walked over to the closet and hung up her coat. "But just so you know, your cat doesn't have your principles."

"I'm amazed to hear it."

"I shut the bedroom door and he made a fuss about wanting in there. I bribed him with a warm scrambled egg and he lost his obsession with our bedroom."

Last night he'd given her joint ownership of the bed. Now he'd expanded it to the entire room. She let it go. "Where is he?"

"Sitting by his food bowl hoping for another scrambled egg."

She laughed. "So you have a partial victory."

"That's all I needed. I told him you'd take care of everything when you came home."

Was he hearing himself? She hadn't *come home.* She'd returned to his cabin. Might as well let that go, too. "Why'd you decide to give him a scrambled egg?"

"Marsh's suggestion. I called him for advice."

"Thanks for that. Must be handy to have a vet in the family."

"You have no idea. Ever since I rescued those pigs I've pestered him for advice constantly."

"That seems fair since he's the one who got you into this."

"It was fair in the beginning, but it's been more than a year. I've promised to pay him once Slim and Pickens start earning their keep." He picked up the insulated bag. "Let's head into the kitchen. I'll get the burgers on the table while you explain to Midnight why he's not allowed in our bedroom."

She followed him into the kitchen and sure enough, Midnight sat directly in front of his bowl. Except the black bowl had been altered. His name had been painted on it in red. "Who added his name?"

"Angie. I asked if she had some red nail polish and when I told her what it was for, she insisted on coming over and doing it herself."

"Good job."

"Oh, and Angie brought a message from Mom. The Wenches are coming over Saturday afternoon at two and they'd love you to drop by."

"That sounds great. It'll be a whole different experience now that I know about your mom."

"You'll have fun with that bunch." He started unpacking the food. "Good, you remembered fries."

"Of course." She picked up Midnight's personalized bowl, got his regular wet food out of the refrigerator and spooned some into the dish. He glanced at it and walked away.

"I see he's not eating that."

"No, but he will if he gets hungry enough."

"I have more eggs."

"No more eggs, at least not for a while. He has to learn that's a special treat, not something he'll get on a regular basis."

Beau gazed at her. "You'll be a really good mom."

"I hope so. If I follow what I remember from how I was raised and get some added wisdom from your mother, I should do a decent job."

"You will." He gestured toward the table. "We're set except for whatever we want to drink. We used to have beer with this meal, but—"

"You can have beer. I'll have..." She doubted he had decaf coffee or tea. "Water's good." She took the chair he'd pulled out for her.

"How about a chocolate shake?"

She glanced up at him, her mouth already watering. "You could make one?"

"It's my second-best talent."

"Oh, is it, now?"

"Wanna know my best talent?"

"I think I already do."

"Betcha don't. I'll show you later. If we're having shakes, I need to make 'em pronto before the burgers get cold. You in?"

"Absolutely. It'll take me back to my childhood. I always ordered one with my burger and fries."

"So did I. Then I bought myself a blender a few years ago." He crossed to the row of cupboards, leaned down and lifted it from a bottom shelf. "Mostly margaritas and daiquiris, I'll admit, but I make chocolate shakes, too, mostly in the summer."

"But it's not summer."

"No, but you're pregnant." He took milk and chocolate syrup from the fridge and vanilla ice cream from the freezer.

"That statement still makes me a little dizzy and disoriented."

"Join the club. I know you're resisting choosing a name, but that would make this kid more real to me." He scooped ice cream into the blender, added milk and syrup, and switched it on.

He'd made a solid point. Putting a name to anything brought it into focus. She waited until he turned off the blender. "You said your mom would come home and announce she was having a baby, and you'd all sit around and decide on a name, but how could you when you didn't know if she'd have a girl or a boy?"

He walked over with two tall glasses filled with creamy chocolate goodness and set one at each place. "I thought about that after telling you the way it went. And I realized she must not have told us until she found out what she'd be having."

"Then we should wait until then."

"Unless we settle on a unisex name." He took the seat catty-corner from her.

"Like Maverick."

"I'll go out on a limb, here. I love that name for our baby. The minute it came up in the discussion with Mom and Sky, I got chills."

"Maybe you were sitting in a draft."

"And maybe it's perfect for him or her." He picked up his shake. "Here's to choosing a name that fits like a glove."

"I'm for that." She touched her glass to his, took a sip and closed her eyes.

"Good?"

She opened her eyes and swallowed. "You know it is."

"Yes, ma'am." He grinned. "I just wanted to hear you say it."

"It's a very good shake."

"That makes me two-for-two. I can make chicken soup and chocolate shakes, a firm foundation of kid-pleasing food items."

She laughed. "You'll get no argument from me."

"Then let the feast begin." He glanced over at Midnight's bowl. "FYI, guess who decided to eat his dinner?"

"Told you." She picked up her deluxe Fluffy Burger, which was almost too big for her mouth, and took a juicy bite. Her hum of appreciation was followed by his, and conversation took a backseat to the meal.

He polished off his burger before she did, but she wasn't far behind. Her fries and shake were almost gone, too.

After draining his glass, he set it down and glanced at her. "That's better."

She nodded. "I was really hungry."

"Me, too, and I didn't want to tackle this next part on an empty stomach."

"What part?" A trickle of unease made her shiver.

"The part where I apologize." He held her gaze. "I should never have said what I did last night. It was selfish and I deeply regret doing it."

"Oh." Her mellow mood evaporated. "Are you…" She paused to take a quick breath. "Are you saying you misspoke?"

"No. I'm saying a better man would have kept the information to himself. We've got enough to figure out without adding that to the mix."

Her heartbeat was unnaturally loud in her ears. "But it's the truth?"

He hesitated. "Yeah." He sighed. "From day one I thought we were a great match. You'd never been engaged, just like me. I figured we were both free spirits."

"And because of that, you expected me to laugh at those jokes on Christmas Eve."

"Afraid so." He grimaced. "Misjudged that one, big time."

Her sense of fairness kicked in. "That's not all on you. I'm pretty sure I didn't say anything about wanting marriage and kids."

"You weren't making fun of the idea, though. I should have picked up on—"

"Why? We'd only been dating a few weeks."

"Good weeks."

"They were." She still had dreams about them. "But we weren't on the same page."

"No, guess not."

"Ironically, I saw my friend's upcoming wedding as a graceful way to find out if you were thinking… what I was thinking."

"Damn." He looked away, his jaw tensing. Then he turned back, his dark eyes filled with anxiety. "You thought I was on the brink of proposing?"

She flushed. "I... um, okay, yes, I did."

With a groan, he buried his face in his hands.

"Please don't blame yourself. I was guilty of misjudging, too."

He looked up, his expression troubled. "You weren't totally wrong."

"What do you mean?"

"I didn't know it then, but now I can see why I told those asinine jokes. I was scared."

"I've figured that out."

"So scared. And yet so close to saying what I said last night."

Leaving him hanging out there, the only one who'd been totally honest, wasn't right. "So was I."

25

"You were in love with me?" Beau's gut clenched.

She nodded.

"Oh, Jess." He reached for her hand and held it between both of his as agony sliced through him. "So I didn't just make you mad. I hurt you."

"We hurt each other."

"I don't care about me."

"I do."

His grip tightened. "But you're not in love with me anymore, right? Of course not. After the way I—"

"I've tried not to be." Her smile trembled. "But I can't seem to—"

"Don't say that. I don't deserve your love."

Her eyes shimmered with unshed tears. "You're a wonderful man. Why wouldn't I love you? We just view our situation... differently."

The tightness in his chest moved up to his throat. "I don't know what to do." He managed to choke out the words. "I want to hold you, but—"

"I want to hold you, too."

"Won't we make everything worse?"

She pushed back her chair. "I'll take that chance if you will."

He stood up so fast he knocked over his chair and scared the cat. Seems he couldn't avoid providing comic relief.

Jess glanced over her shoulder as Midnight streaked out of the room. "Probably going under the sofa. That's where he hides in my house."

"Then let's vamoose before he comes back out." He took her hand and headed straight for the bedroom. Finding solace in each other's arms was probably a huge mistake, but he was willing to make it.

He undressed her slowly, tenderly. Then he put himself in her hands. She took her time, too, pausing every so often to kiss a spot she'd uncovered.

She loved him. Now all the soft glances and warm smiles made sense. Her decision to stay with him did not. She'd shown incredible courage in the face of certain pain. That was humbling.

When at last he drew her down to the smooth sheets, he touched her with reverence. He didn't trust himself to speak. Those three words he didn't have the right to say were sure to come tumbling out.

She remained silent, too, but her luminous gaze held his from the moment he thrust deep until she cried out in the grip of her release. He followed soon after, the tremors wracking his body, her quiet tears breaking his heart.

* * *

Beau couldn't fall asleep. Judging from Jess's shallow breathing, she'd been able to drift off. That was a blessing. Good for her and good for the baby.

At some point her cat meowed at the door. Beau eased out of bed, quietly gathered his clothes and blocked Midnight from going in as he went out. He gently closed the door and carried his clothes into the living room. The cat trotted after him.

"Good kitty. We need to let her sleep, okay?"

Midnight hopped up on the sofa and began grooming himself while Beau got dressed.

"I'm gonna clean up the dinner dishes, kitty. You're welcome to keep me company." He walked barefoot across the smooth wood floor into the kitchen, Midnight at his heels. Thank goodness he'd installed radiant heat from the get-go. Pricey, but worth it in the winter.

Yeah, he'd created exactly the sort of place he'd dreamed of — a bachelor pad with all the amenities. The cabin could easily accommodate a female companion, but a baby would make it feel crowded.

"I might as well admit it, kitty." He picked up the dishes from the table and carried them over to the sink, careful not to trip over the cat, who was making figure eights between his legs. "I don't know what the hell I'm doing."

Midnight put his front paws on the bottom cupboard door, lifted his furry face and meowed.

"I see your dish is empty. I also know what you're begging for. Jess might not like it if I fixed you another scrambled egg, and she's the boss."

Midnight responded by walking over to his bowl and sitting beside it.

"You're a stubborn little cuss. You remind me of those pigs. I wonder if you'd get along with 'em." He returned to his task. "I don't see it as a natural pairing, but you never know. Opposites attract and all that."

"Like us?"

He glanced toward the doorway. Jess leaned against the arched opening wearing the forest green robe she'd brought but hadn't worn. Her nightgown was still folded in the dresser drawer, too.

"I'm sorry." He closed the dishwasher and dried his hands. "I made too much noise."

"You didn't. I heard you leave. I thought you might find a way to bribe Midnight and then come back to bed."

"The scrambled egg's my only trick and I didn't want to give him that without asking you."

"Another sign you'll be a terrific dad. You listen."

"I haven't always, but in this situation—"

"In this situation, you shine."

"I'm not so sure that I—"

"It's true, Beau. You kid around with the adults in your life, but put a creature or a person in your care, and you give it everything you have."

"Thank you."

"You're welcome. I was lying in there thinking about the parenting example your mother has set, not to mention Buck and Marybeth's influence. You were made for fatherhood. Heck, you probably helped take care of Rance and Lucky when they were babies."

"I did." He was afraid to ask where she was going with this.

"You invited me here to prove you'll be a trustworthy father."

"Yes."

"I'd be a fool to doubt it. You're so good with Slim and Pickens. You've gone above and beyond for my cat. You've had experience with your little brothers. You'll be a terrific dad. You don't have to keep proving it to me."

"All right." He tensed. The other shoe was about to drop.

"There's no reason for me to stay."

There it was. Grief threatened to swamp him. He gulped it down. She was right to go. He was wrong to want her to stay. "I... uh... thought we'd go riding this weekend."

"I know you wanted to do that, but is hanging out together in this kind of intimate setting a good idea?"

He had no answer.

"It'll just make things harder for both of us. But I'll come back for Angie's party."

He nodded. If he could mute the screaming in his head, he'd get the point she was making. "When... when did you want to shove off?"

"As soon as I can get dressed and pack up."

"Now? It's the middle of the night."

"I can't sleep and clearly you can't, either. We've said everything there is to say. We..." Her breath caught and she looked away. "Making love isn't going to solve anything."

"I know." Only one thing would make her stay, and he couldn't take that leap. Not now. Maybe not ever. The steel door slammed down, leaving him cold and alone.

If he didn't get moving, he was liable to break down and bawl. "I'll help you with Midnight's stuff."

"Thank you."

They worked efficiently and in silence. Well, they were silent, but Midnight pitched a fit when they tried to load him into the carrier. As a last resort, Beau scrambled an egg and set it in a small dish at the back of the carrier. Mission accomplished.

He shoved his feet into his boots but didn't bother with his coat and hat while he helped her load the car. The numbing cold was exactly what he craved. It matched the icicles forming in his chest.

Too soon everything was packed neatly into her SUV. She gave him a quick hug and slid into the driver's seat. "Thank you for—"

"No thanks required. Just so long as you left a hefty tip for the housekeeper."

She gave him a ghost of a smile. "Actually, I didn't. I thought he'd be insulted."

"Good call. Listen, you'll have to unload all this. I could follow you and help—"

"I won't unload it tonight. Just my cat. The rest can wait until morning."

"Okay, then. Drive safe. Will you text me when you get there?"

"Yes."

"See you for the party." He closed the door and backed a few steps away so she wouldn't have to worry about running over his foot. A broken foot would give him something else to think about, though.

He stayed where he was until the red glow of her taillights disappeared around the bend. Pathetic fool that he was, he gave her some time to change her mind, turn around and come back.

When his teeth began to chatter so bad he was in danger of biting his tongue, he abandoned his post. Then again, a bleeding tongue would also give him something else to think about.

Craving a painful injury to distract himself from mooning over Jess probably wasn't a healthy response. Damned if he could come up with a healthy one, though. The booze in his fridge was calling his name.

He forced himself to climb the steps and walk into the house. The very empty house. What now? Go out in back and wake up the pigs? They wouldn't appreciate that.

He discarded the urge to tie one on. He had two client appointments in the morning. He owed the folks and the horses a decent session. Climbing into his bed was out, though. Might be quite a while before he slept there again.

Walking to the closet, he took out his duster, stretched out on the sofa and pulled the duster over him. Maybe he'd pretend he was on an overnight trail ride.

Or maybe he'd just lie there and stare at the unlocked front door. Jess might still come through it.

26

Jess gave it the old college try when she got ready for work in the morning, but makeup could only do so much. She wasn't surprised when her dad called her back to his office and shut the door.

She'd brought her phone in case her ten o'clock interview called to cancel. Right. Keeping her phone with her at all times had nothing to do with the possibility that Beau might call or text.

Her dad pushed his glasses to the top of his head. "Okay, Jessie-girl. What gives?"

Jessie-girl. He only called her that when he was super worried. "I'm fine."

"Really? You look like hell."

"Thanks, Dad."

"You know me, kid. I tell it like it is. What happened?"

"I left Rowdy Ranch last night and I… didn't sleep much once I got home."

"Weren't you supposed to stay through Valentine's Day?"

"That was the original plan, but—"

"If that guy has caused you pain, I'm driving out there." His eyes took on a steely glint. "I warned him if he ever—"

"It's not Beau's fault. Or mine. We made assumptions about each other and we were both dead wrong. Based on those assumptions, we allowed ourselves to..." Emotions crowded her chest and sucked the air from her lungs.

"Fall in love?" Her dad's tone was the gentle one he'd used when she tumbled off her bike or had a fight with one of her childhood friends.

She nodded. "And there's no good solution. He's skittish about marriage and I can't just hang around in some loosey-goosey co-habitation arrangement on the off chance he gets over it. Even if I did agree to that, his cabin isn't suitable. There's only one—"

"The cabin is just details, sweetie. Did you choose to leave or did he suggest it?"

"I chose to leave."

"Because he was being mean?"

"No! He's never been anything but wonderful. But I was mostly there to evaluate his fitness as a dad. I've done that and I'm convinced he'll be great at it."

"Was he okay with you leaving?"

Tears pushed at the back of her eyes. "He was miserable. But dragging this out was—"

"So he wanted you to stay the whole seven days?"

"I'm sure he did, but I couldn't see the point."

"Because the solution is buried in a ton of crap, Jess. That boy's still trying to figure out what he wants. And whether he's brave enough to go after it."

"If you're right, I'm glad I left last night. If he's fighting his inner demons, I don't want to get caught in the—" Her phone chimed. "Excuse me a minute. That's him."

"Pretend I'm not here."

That made her smile. "I'll put the call on speaker, so you can see he's not a villain." She tapped a button on her phone. "Hey, Beau."

"Hey, Jess." His voice filled the office and gave her goosebumps. "Sorry to bother you at work."

"No worries." She winked at her dad. "My dad says hi."

"He does? He's not ready to clean my clock?"

"No, I'm not, son."

"Sir, I'm so sorry for anything I've—"

"He knows, Beau." Her throat hurt. "I've explained there's no blame, here. Why did you call?"

"Mom would love you to come out tomorrow afternoon when the Wenches are here, even though you're not—"

"I can do that."

"Thanks. I told her I'd call. I don't want you to worry that you'll have to see me. I won't be around."

She glanced down at her shoes, not wanting her dad to see the tears she blinked away. "You don't have to avoid me."

"I don't plan to make a habit of it. I just... need a little time."

"Okay. Thanks for the call. Talk to you later. Bye." She hung up, took a quick breath and faced her dad.

He gazed at her, his expression grim. "That's one troubled man."

"I know. He's... we..."

"I hope you haven't totally written him off."

"I can't. He's the father of my child."

"And a good guy."

"You really do like him, don't you?"

"Yes." He held up his hands, palms out. "But this is your call."

"You want me to give him some rope, though."

"Only if that works for you, sweetheart." He paused. "So you'll be meeting with the Wenches tomorrow afternoon?"

"I will."

"I think it's great that they're reaching out. Maybe they'll want you to join. Sort of a legacy thing."

"If they do, I'd be thrilled."

"I remember them meeting on a weeknight, though, not Saturday afternoon."

"I get the impression this isn't a regular book club meeting. I think it's about me and the baby."

"Makes sense. They're sort of... filling in." He looked away and swallowed.

Stepping closer, she wrapped her arms around him. "Nobody could take her place, Dad."

He hugged her close. "No." His voice was thick. "But I love them for trying."

* * *

Since moving back last summer, Jess had run into the Wenches in town several times, singly and sometimes in pairs. They'd always greeted her with enthusiasm and talked vaguely about getting together for coffee or drinks.

That hadn't happened. Maybe a big-city reporter had made them nervous, especially after she'd come out to interview Desiree.

The drive to Rowdy Ranch wasn't a feel-good trip by any means, but she was eager to see the Wenches now that they could talk freely after years of secrecy.

Marybeth met her at the door and pulled her into a hug that nearly squeezed the breath out of her. The woman was tiny, but she had the grip of a lumberjack. "Oh, honey, I'm so sorry. I had such hope that my soup would do the trick."

Jess stepped back and pulled air into her lungs. "It's fabulous soup. If any soup could have worked a miracle, it would be that one." She took off her coat.

"Here, I'll take that." Marybeth hung it up. "You do know that boy's in love with you."

"I'm in love with him, too. But I want marriage and, if I'm lucky, more children. That's not his thing."

"It's got something to do with his father." Marybeth sighed. "I'd lay money on it."

"Did you know him?"

She shook her head. "Before my time. Desiree hired Buck and me after Beau's dad left.

She needed help around here and she also felt her boys would benefit from a male role model, someone steady and kind. That's my Buck, for sure."

"Clearly everyone adores him. And you."

"We adore them right back. Couldn't have kids of our own, so this was heaven's way of setting things right. Anyway, I've kept you long enough. The Wenches are chomping at the bit. Just go on into the library and prepare to get mugged."

Jess hurried toward the library and the welcome sound of laughter. She could do with some good cheer.

When she walked into the library, five women leaped from their chairs and whooped with joy as they ran toward her, arms outstretched. She caught a glimpse of Desiree's grin before she was smothered in a group hug amid cries of welcome, congratulations and questions about the baby.

"Okay, that's enough. Everybody back off." It sounded like Annette's well-modulated voice, one that matched her style — classic clothes and hair tamed with a silver clip. "We need to give this poor girl some air."

"Good idea." That was Nancy, who favored a bouffant do and was sporting a tiara. "Cindy, your elbow's in my boob."

"Beg pardon, Your Royal Rackness." Cindy stepped away and executed a courtly bow. She kept her hair short and spiky. Today it was pink.

"I need some air, too." Teresa, her gray hair an easy style of loose natural curls, wrinkled her nose. "Colleen, you're wearing that smelly lotion *again*?"

"It makes my skin soft as a baby's butt." Colleen, perpetually blonde, pushed back the sleeve of her red sweater. "Just feel that."

"No thanks. I might get some on me."

"All right, gang, get it together." Nancy straightened her tiara. "Stand on either side of me and make a line. Jess, you face me. It's time to administer the oath."

"What oath?" And why was Nancy in charge and not Desiree?

"The one we created twenty-five years ago." Annette handed Nancy a slim leather-bound book.

Nancy held it out to Jess. "Put your left hand on the book and raise your right."

"What is it?" Jess leaned over to read the spine.

"An uncirculated copy of Louis L'Amour's first story, *Hondo.*"

Jess straightened and smiled at Desiree as she laid her hand on the textured surface. "Now I understand the name of your bookstore. L'Amour must be a role model."

"Absolutely."

Nancy took a breath. "Let's begin. Repeat after me. I solemnly swear."

"I solemnly swear."

"To speak the truth, the whole truth and nothing but the truth about M.R. Morrison's work."

Jess repeated the phrase.

"Whether the plot is crappy or brilliant."

She glanced at the sparkle in Desiree's eyes. This was shaping up to be a blast. "Whether the plot is crappy or brilliant."

"Whether the characters are cardboard cutouts or fully-realized individuals we're dying to meet."

She grinned as she recited that part.

"I make this pledge in the name of Louis L'Amour."

Jess cleared the laughter from her throat and made the pledge.

"By the power vested in me as the presiding Grand High Priestess of the Order of L'Amour, I now pronounce you, Jessica Ann Hartmann, a lifetime member of Wenches Who Read."

A cheer went up from the group.

Jess had received several honors, both in school and in broadcasting, but this beat them all.

Nancy looked at her. "Any questions?"

"Only one. You're a fabulous High Priestess, but why you and not Desiree?"

"Because it's my turn. We rotate the position every quarter."

"Then I'll get a turn?"

"Yes, ma'am."

"And I get to wear the tiara?"

"Goes with the job."

"Cool. I can't wait."

"Okay, time to take our seats. Jess, you're there." She gestured toward the green chair.

"Thank you! It's the same chair I picked when I came to interview you, Desiree." She glanced in her direction. "I love that one."

Desiree held her gaze. "So did your mother."

Jess froze. "Are you saying that was…" Light-headedness made her wobble.

Nancy grabbed her arm to steady her. "Easy, honey."

Heart racing, Jess surveyed the rainbow of chairs. "Each of you has a specific chair?"

"We do." Colleen pointed to the red one. "That's mine." She walked over and sat in it.

Jess looked around the semi-circle. Each woman had settled into her chair — violet for Desiree, indigo for Annette, orange for Teresa, blue for Cindy and yellow for Nancy.

She took a shaky breath. "You've left my mother's chair empty all this time?"

"Couldn't find anyone worthy to fill it," Desiree said, her voice husky. "Until now."

Tears rolling down her cheeks, Jess choked out a watery thank you.

"Aw, heck," Cindy left her seat. "We gotta have another group hug."

Nancy stood, too. "When you're right, you're right."

Once again, Jess was enveloped by the loving arms of her mother's best friends. It wasn't like having her mom back, but it was darned close.

27

Around midday, Beau set out on Champion. He'd kept the big bay in shape through the winter with short rides and some time on the lunge line. But his horse needed a longer ride to work the kinks out.

Yeah, this was for Champion's benefit. It had nothing to do with avoiding any chance of encountering Jess. He stayed out until twilight and finally brought an eager Champion back for his supper.

Sky and Buck were delivering hay flakes when he led Champion down the barn aisle to his stall. "Evening, gentlemen."

"And the weary traveler returns," Buck called out.

"Timed it just right. You're almost done."

Buck snorted and continued with his task.

Sky gave him a glance as he grabbed a hay flake from the wheelbarrow in the aisle. "Wondered when you'd show up. Buck and I were debating whether to send out a search party."

"Ah, you knew I'd be here. Me and my horse never miss a meal." He led Champion into his stall, quickly unsaddled him and took off his bridle.

Sky brought in a flake of hay and dumped it in the hay net. "How long you been out there?"

"Left around noon."

"Long ride."

"I'm about to fetch the grooming tote, if that's what you were hinting at."

"No, little brother, I wasn't. Did you take your phone with you? I only ask because Mom said she texted you and you didn't answer."

"I didn't take it."

"Dammit, Beau, you can't be going out there in the dead of winter without your phone. What if—"

"A mountain lion fancies a snack? A hungry grizzly comes out of hibernation? A pair of eagles goes rogue and pecks out our eyes? Or God forbid we meet a snowshoe hare. Have you seen the front teeth on those things?"

"Go ahead. Make jokes. Some folks here were worried. That's on you."

Beau breathed deep as his brother's anger added to the lump of misery in his gut. "Sorry, bro. You're right. I'll call her the minute I get home."

Sky pulled his phone out of his pocket and hit a button. "Call her now."

He took the phone and made the call. "Hey, Mom."

"Beau? Why are you calling from Sky's phone? Are you okay? What happened to your—"

"I apologize. My bad. I needed to get away and I didn't take my phone. I'm in the barn and Sky loaned me his so I could call. I'm sorry I worried you."

"I forgive you, but I thought we all agreed that cell phones are a blessing, not a curse. Nobody knew which way you went. If you'd ended up hurt out on the trail, we wouldn't have known where to look. You could have… well, I don't even want to say what might have happened."

"I screwed up. I won't do it again."

"See that you don't."

"I won't, I promise. Anyway, Sky said you texted me. What about?"

"Two things. First of all, the Wenches gained another member today."

"Ahh, good call." At last, some happy news. "I'm sure she was beside herself."

"Overwhelmed, but delighted. I'm glad I didn't tell her during the interview last fall that she'd chosen her mother's chair. Finding it out today had more impact."

"She cried." His heart was too big for his chest right now.

"She did. We all did. She'll be an awesome addition. I can't wait to finish this next book and get her input. She's so sharp. She'll keep us all on our toes."

He couldn't resist. "You're welcome."

"You're taking credit? I thought it was the cat's fault."

"He was an accomplice, but I'm the key man in this story. She never would have asked me out. I started the ball rolling, so to speak."

"To continue your metaphor, the ball's going downhill."

"Bound to happen. Gravity works."

"Aerodynamics overcomes gravity."

"You lost me."

"I need a couple of hours of your time tomorrow afternoon. Supposed to be a nice day. A bit of a breeze."

He went from being lost to a jump ahead of her. "Mom, I don't think that's a good—"

"We need to have a talk. Let's go fly a kite."

"I checked that kite online recently. It's worth a fortune. Hand-painted silk, finely crafted bamboo. I don't want to risk it."

"Beau McLintock, you risked your *life* by not taking your phone today. You can damn well risk that freaking *kite*. Meet me at the house at one-thirty."

"Yes, ma'am."

* * *

Beau parked at the house at one-twenty-six. Typically his mom would rally the troops for something like this. But her truck was the only one there.

When he walked in, Sam didn't run to greet him and when he called out, hers was the only voice that answered. "Come on back. I already have the stepladder."

He left his jacket and hat on as he walked toward his childhood bedroom. Once he had the kite, he wasn't letting go until it was airborne.

"Where's Sam?"

"I closed him in my bedroom while we get this thing down. I'll let him go outside with us." She stood, hands on hips, gazing up at the ceiling. "How'd we get it up there in the first place?"

"Buck. I wasn't tall enough." He met her determined gaze. "How about having this talk over a cup of coffee in the kitchen?"

"That lacks gravitas. We're going to fly this kite together, Beau. It's an appropriate activity for a discussion we desperately need to have."

After more than thirty years of interaction with his mother, he knew better than to argue when her words sounded as if they'd been hammered into shape on Bret and Gil's forge.

"Care to tell me what this discussion will be about?"

"Not yet. Once we get the kite in the air."

"And I can't escape?"

She laughed. "Something like that."

Taking down the kite was a dusty, two-person job that left them both sneezing.

His mother blew her nose. "How long has that thing been up there?"

"He sent it for my tenth birthday, so more than twenty years."

"It's a wonder it hasn't disintegrated."

"Like I said, this is museum-quality, built to last." He held it carefully in his arms. "Are you sure you want to—"

"Lives are on the line. Speaking of lines, where's the kite string and the thingamabob it goes on?"

"Umm, try the bottom shelf, far right side."

She crouched down. "I don't... oh, here it is. I can't imagine how you find anything on these shelves."

"I don't have to. I just shove things in and leave them there, except for this kite. I wanted to see it stretched out."

"It's impressive, all right. Should look great in the sky."

"But not so great tangled in a pine tree."

"You won't let it drop into a tree. You've flown kites hundreds of times."

"Not this kind." But now that it wasn't hanging from the ceiling out of reach, he had the urge to see what it could do.

He waited while she let Sam out and put on her coat and knit cap. Then she held the door for him and kept a grip on Sam's collar.

"Thanks." He walked outside and glanced up at the sky, a brilliant blue with a few puffy clouds. "Perfect kite-flying day."

"Told you." She turned Sam loose and he pranced around Beau, eyes bright and tail waving.

"I was thinking the pasture, but Sky and Buck turned the horses out."

"How about right here in the space between the house and the barn? You kids used to fly kites here all the time."

"They were a lot smaller than this." He studied the terrain. "But, yeah, this might be as good a spot as any."

"It really is a perfect gift for a boy who lives in Big Sky Country."

"Uh-huh."

"What was that?"

"That was a half-assed yes, ma'am."

"Ah, Beau." She chuckled. "You're the gift, son." She located the end of the kite string. "Where does this go?"

"On the kite."

She laughed. "No kidding? I thought we'd fly it with the strength of our minds."

"Oh, we should do that, too. But we also need a string. There's a metal ring right there." He held the kite so she could see it.

"Aha. It's coming back to me. I need to make a loop thingy so it'll stay on." She secured the string. "All set. Take her out and toss her up."

"Once the wind catches it, you'll need to make sure the line's nice and taut."

"Don't worry. I'll keep it aloft until you get back. Then she's all yours."

"How long since you've flown a kite?"

"About the same amount of time as you." She gave him a smile. "Trust me, son. I've got this."

His gaze narrowed. "Are we doing a team-building exercise?"

"Such a smart boy."

"Huh." He turned, his boots crunching on the frozen ground as he walked the kite a few yards away, Sam close on his heels. She slowly fed him line from the spool. *Team building.* She'd been big on it when he and his siblings were growing up. Could be why they were such a tight bunch, now.

The breeze picked up. Good time to launch this sucker. He turned. "Ready?"

"Ready when you are!"

He heaved the kite in the air and the string tightened immediately as she backed away, her touch exactly right. Sam barked with excitement as the kite began its climb skyward.

His mom spooled out the line like a pro. Hand-painted silk, brilliant in the sunlight, fluttered and danced above him. Gorgeous. That kite wanted to fly.

"Are you gonna come take this or what?"

"Oh! Sorry. Come on, Sam." He trotted back to her, the collie keeping in step. "I got distracted by how beautiful it is." He took the spool, careful to maintain the tension.

"Looks way better in the air than hanging from the ceiling."

"Point taken. Should have done this years ago."

"But you're doing it now. Thanks for going along with my plan."

He glanced at her. "Now comes the fun part. Gonna tell me what prompted this team building-slash-discussion?"

"I had a chat with Jess yesterday after the Wenches left."

"Figured you might." He glanced around for Sam, who'd lost interest in the kite and was exploring, nose to the ground, reading the doggie news of the day.

"She told me you're wary of marriage because it'll tie you down."

He shifted uncomfortably. "I did say that."

"Where'd you come up with that?"

"You, I guess. You're not married. You're a free spirit, like me."

"And I'm the most tied-down person you'll ever meet."

"But—"

"I can't believe such a thing is genetic, but you sound exactly like Steven."

"Who's Steven?"

"Your father. Steven Jacobson."

"Oh." His gut tightened. "I think you told me once. Then I forgot. His name was never on the packages. Just some company name."

"His company. He's a successful importer."

"So that's why he travels all over?"

"He travels all over because that's his passion. He found a way to turn his passion into a money-making venture."

"Good for him."

"You sound bitter, son."

"If he's so damned successful, he could afford to come back once in a while."

"Not so easy for him. He was raised by a drunken father who beat him. He was afraid he'd repeat the pattern, so he doesn't trust himself. No kids for him."

"So I was a mistake." He'd suspected that, but having it confirmed was—

"You were *not* a mistake! None of my children were mistakes. Steven and I adored each other. But he wanted to travel. I had a child and wanted another so they could be buddies. Steven agreed to help me with that. Once I conceived, he set off on his next adventure."

"That doesn't explain why he stayed gone. He couldn't beat me up now." The head of the dragon kite, the size of a truck tire on the ground, now looked smaller than a basketball. The tail rose straight up above it. Spectacular.

"I've asked him to come, but he's nervous that you won't like him, that he won't know how to act or what to say."

"That makes two of us."

"Do you *want* him to come?"

"I don't know." He sighed. "And even if I do, you said he's reluctant, so—"

"But he's going to be a grandfather."

He stared at her. "No, he's not."

"Yes, he is. Technically."

"*Technically*. But you don't get to call yourself a grandparent because thirty years ago you—"

"Watch out for the kite. It's—"

"Yikes." He tugged on the string and shortened it a little. Sam gave it a glance as it swooped down before regaining its position. Then he went back to exploring.

"Thanks for the warning. I don't want it to crash."

"Hm."

"And not because he gave it to me. It's a great kite."

"Tell that to someone who hasn't watched you hang onto every birthday gift he sent. I think he'd come if I said you wanted him to."

His chest ached. "I need to check with Jess. She gets a say in this."

His mom smiled. "Well said. He wouldn't stay long, so no worries on that score. Like I mentioned, he has a fear of being tied down."

"So do you."

"What gave you that idea?"

"You're not married. I get the situation with Sky's dad and now I know about mine, but what about the others? Wasn't anybody—"

"They were not. Each time I thought maybe, and each time we came to a mutual decision that we didn't have the right combo for the long haul."

"I've never heard that. I didn't know."

"Now you do. And in this grand experiment of mine, I've gained a ton of experience in matters of the heart. In my educated opinion, you and Jess have what it takes for the long haul."

"She definitely does, but I'm... I'm not sure what I am."

"No? You built a beautiful cabin on Rowdy Ranch so you could be less than ten minutes from me and each of your siblings. You adopted two pigs that require daily attention. You've created a profitable business and based it locally in Wagon Train. You have the wanderlust of a turtle."

"Hey, I like to travel."

"When was the last time you were on a plane?"

"Um, I—"

"Five years ago when you went to that Buck Brannaman clinic in Denver to get inspiration for your business. Face it, Beau, you're not a rolling stone like your dad. You're a homebody, a poster boy for marriage and family."

He got chills. That couldn't be true, could it? "If you've had trouble all these years finding the right person, what makes you think I've suddenly hit the jackpot?"

"Because you're just that lucky, Beau McLintock."

28

Jess figured she wouldn't see Beau until Angie's birthday party on Tuesday night, but he surprised the heck out of her by calling Monday morning and inviting her to have lunch at the Buffalo.

She put him on hold and checked with Monica. "Beau's asked me to lunch. Do you want the noon or one slot? Your choice."

"I'll go you one better. I'll order my lunch delivered and eat at my desk. Go ahead and take two hours. He wouldn't ask if it wasn't important."

Her stomach churned. "Probably not. Thank you. I owe you a two-hour lunch whenever you want to take one."

"Here's my dirty little secret. I love being here. I'm a news hound, always sniffing around waiting for something big to break."

Jess smiled. "I'm kind of the same. Printer's ink in my blood."

"And I prefer a small-town weekly to a big-city daily. I love reporting local news."

"Backatcha, Monica. I'm proud to share the newsroom with you."

"Same here, toots. Now tell your guy you're available for lunch."

Your guy. Not true, but Monica was an optimist who was convinced Jess and Beau would come to an understanding.

Jess agreed to meet Beau at noon and returned to her latest project, digging up historical tidbits on Wagon Train. The town would celebrate its one hundred and twenty-fifth anniversary in two years and her dad had asked her to start gathering material for a commemorative book.

Good thing she'd trained herself to work no matter what. Any good journalist needed that skill and she'd honed it during her stint in Philadelphia. Without it, she'd have spent the morning obsessing about why Beau had asked her to lunch.

The Buffalo was only a five-minute walk from the *Sentinel* office and the weather had taken a turn for the better. She left her knit hat in the office for the quick trip down the street.

Once again, she'd forgotten that Valentine's Day was the following day. Approaching the front door of the Buffalo quickly reminded her. A heart-shaped wreath of pink, white and red carnations hung on the front door.

Inside, the life-sized wooden buffalo at the entrance wore a crown of red and white flowers. He groaned his usual *welcooome to the buuufalooo*, and then added *beeee myyyy vaaaalintiiiine?* Sounded like a bull who'd just downed a vat of whisky.

"Sure will, Buffy." In high school she'd circulated a petition to name him and Buffy was the biggest vote-getter. But the owner hadn't promoted the name so it hadn't caught on. Maybe her dad would let her mount another campaign through the *Sentinel.*

The interior of the tavern continued the Valentine theme with shiny red hearts hanging from the ceiling and carnations in bud vases on every table. Nothing like in-your-face romance when she was meeting her ex.

He'd claimed a two-top in the far corner. She appreciated the thought. The location should reduce the number of folks who'd come over to congratulate them on the happy event. Maybe they'd assume the lovebirds wanted privacy.

When he spotted her, he stood. His gentlemanly manners never failed to charm her. Hooking his thumbs in his belt loops, he held her gaze as the distance between them disappeared. He wasn't smiling, but he didn't look upset, either. Just... thoughtful.

He'd worn one of her favorite yoked shirts, a forest-green with pearl snaps. The deep shade complimented his coloring and the snug fit emphasized his broad shoulders and muscular chest. Dammit, he was a good-looking cowboy. The sight of him left her breathless and shaky. How long before that stopped happening?

"Thanks for having lunch with me."

"You're welcome. I was surprised when you—"

"I wanted to talk about something that came up yesterday. This seemed like a good option." He broke eye contact and pulled out her chair. "I'm glad you could make it. How soon do you have to be back?"

She slid into the chair. "Monica offered to cover for me. We have until two."

"Nice of her." He scooted her in and took his seat across from her. "What do you want?"

You. She picked up the menu and pretended to consult it. "A burger and shake." Wait, not a good idea to reprise their last meal together. "Or maybe—"

"I'll have the same." He glanced up as Rance came over, all smiles. "Aren't you supposed to be behind the bar, little brother?"

"I'll head on back after I take your order, bro. Just wanted to say hi to Jess. Nice to see you again, ma'am."

She returned his smile. "Same here, Rance."

"Did he tell you he and Mom took the kite out yesterday?"

"No, he sure didn't. That's—"

"She just got here, Rance."

"I know, but it's big news. I mean, twenty years hanging from your bedroom ceiling, with all of us begging you to fly it and—"

"Twenty years?" Jess looked across the table. "That *is* a big deal. How come you—"

"I was planning to tell you. But my little brother jumped the—"

"Is my employee harassing you folks?" Clint appeared and wrapped an arm around Rance's shoulders. "Correct me if I'm wrong, bro, but I believe your job description is *bartender.*"

"I was just gonna get their order real quick."

"Did you get it?"

"Not yet. Can you believe he didn't tell her about the kite first thing? That's a major—"

"Rance." Clint turned him in the direction of the bar. "Drink orders are coming in. Go tend bar before Tyra notices and asks me again why I hired you."

Jess glanced at him. "How do you like working for her?"

"She's terrific." He gave Rance a gentle push toward the bar and turned back to her. "A real powerhouse."

"I believe it. When I was a freshman, she ruled the senior class — head cheerleader, class president, valedictorian."

Clint nodded. "That's my boss. A high achiever. Rance needs to stay sharp if he wants to keep his job. And since he neglected to take your order, what'll you have?"

"Burgers and chocolate shakes for both of us," Beau said.

"Got it." Clint glanced at Jess. "Make sure he tells you about that kite."

"I will."

"Your food will be up in no time. Nice seeing you, Jess." He left, calling out greetings to customers as he passed by their tables on the way to the kitchen.

Jess gazed at Beau. "So. The kite."

"The kite."

"Was it fun, flying it?"

"Matter of fact, it was. But I should've known she had an ulterior motive."

"Us?"

"In a way. Seems when you told her yesterday that I didn't want to get tied down—"

"She asked me point blank. I didn't think she'd be surprised you felt that way, but she was."

"When you told her my reason, she had a *déjà vu* moment. My dad used to say the same thing."

"That's not something that could be passed down genetically."

"But kids pick up on stuff. I looked at my parents and made up my story. My mom's never married, despite having plenty of opportunity. My dad clearly didn't want a wife or kids. I figured they knew what they were doing, staying away from that institution."

"I can see how you'd think that." Her pulse rate picked up. Had he changed his mind?

"I'd also concluded I was an unplanned pregnancy, like Sky. And our baby."

"We know it happens." Since he'd switched topics, maybe he hadn't changed his opinion.

"It does, but it turns out I *was* planned. My dad agreed to father a child with mom because he loved her and she wanted another baby soon. Her kids would have each other as playmates, which was good for us. And good for her, because she'd have more time to write."

"But if your dad loved her, why didn't he stay?"

"He had a rotten father and thought he'd be the same. And he does love traveling. Mom had no such plans."

"Why didn't she tell you this before?"

"She tried a few times. That's when I learned that jokes can derail any conversation I don't want to have. I was afraid she'd tell me I was an accident my dad never wanted, so I diverted every discussion. Until yesterday."

She let out a happy sigh. "I'm glad she made you listen to that story."

"Me, too. I don't resent him like I did, but it's not like we have a relationship. Evidently now he feels awkward about meeting me after all these years."

"Do you want to meet him?"

"Maybe. Mom thinks he might come to see the baby. After all, technically he'll be a grandfather."

Her breath caught. "So he will. I didn't think of that."

"I want you to weigh in, though. I don't know my dad at all and my mom hasn't seen him in thirty years, although they've talked on the phone. If you have any problem with inviting him here, I won't do it."

She blinked. "You won't?"

"This baby is ours, not mine. As the mother, you have the right to turn thumbs down on this idea. I won't lie, I'm damned nervous about it, myself. If you—"

"Beau, you should invite him. I'm sure it'll be fine. And if for some reason it's not fine, our baby will be surrounded by eight ferocious uncles, two mighty aunts, one protective grandpa and one kickass grandma."

"You forgot us — one formidable mom and one fearsome dad."

"Exactly."

"When you describe all that backup, I don't know why I'm nervous about having him come. August is a great time to visit Montana."

"You could fly that kite while he's here."

"We could, at that. By the way, if the weather holds, Angie's asked if she can fly it tomorrow as a birthday treat. It would cut into your work day, but if you could come out a little early, like around four, you could see it, maybe take a turn."

"Sounds like fun." And wasn't this what she'd ultimately wanted? That they could interact as friends? "I'll check with Dad."

"It'd be great if he could come with you. If you don't mind, I'll walk back with you and ask him to the party myself."

"I don't mind, and he might want to come, but..." She lowered her voice and leaned closer. "Is that a good idea? He's a seasoned newspaper man. Aren't you worried about—"

"It's smarter to start including him than to keep him at arm's length. Then he might get suspicious that the family's hiding something."

"True." She settled back in her chair and studied him, never a chore. "I think this is the longest conversation we've ever had without you cracking a joke."

He smiled. "Guess I didn't feel like derailing any of it."

"That's nice, Beau."
"Yeah, it is." He held her gaze. "Very nice."

29

Birthdays were a big deal at Rowdy Ranch. Beau always enjoyed honoring the day a member of the family had been born. And after the talk with his mom, Angie's twenty-fourth year glowed brighter than any in the past.

The weather dictated birthday activities, and Angie had lucked out. The morning was sunny enough for a family trail ride with a packed lunch included. Miraculously, everybody's schedules meshed.

The birthday girl led the group, her hat decorated with ribbons. Her mother fell in behind her, followed by Penny. The brothers rode in birth order. Buck brought up the rear, right behind Marybeth. Sam pranced around and between the fourteen riders, clearly thrilled with the program.

Beau's place behind Sky held more significance than ever before. He belonged there. His mom had chosen to bring him into the world to strengthen her little family unit.

Traditionally, trail rides prompted the retelling of family stories, mostly the hilarious ones. Beau contributed his share, but the urge to be the chief entertainer had faded since that conversation on Sunday.

After the ride, the rest of the family kept Angie occupied while he set up a birthday pig race in the corral—a row of twenty-four colorful flags marking the course and a birthday banner at the finish line. He'd decked out Slim and Pickens in party hats, which might or might not stay on. He texted his Mom. *Ready.*

Everyone came out of the house, Angie in the lead. When she caught sight of the corral and the pigs in hats, she laughed and clapped her hands. "So *cute*! What a great idea!"

"Want to announce the race?"

"Can I?"

"Why not?" He'd never turned the job over to anyone, but she'd watched him race those pigs several times.

"Then I'll do it."

He gave her treats to tuck in her pockets before she took her position at the finish line. Grinning like crazy, she curled her fist into a semblance of a mic like he always did. She called the race exactly as he would have, chortling out *Pickens wins, Pickens wins* at the end. Neither hat made it the whole way.

While the rest of the family cheered and he joined Angie in giving the pigs scratches and belly rubs, Andy Hartmann's truck pulled into the parking lot near the house. Jess was here. Beau's heart lodged in his throat.

The family rushed over to welcome Jess and her dad. Beau meandered over, staying at the fringe of the crowd so he could absorb the joyful scene and the beauty of Jess, laughing at a comment from Rance, hugging Angie and wishing her happy birthday, hugging his mom and saying something that made her smile.

Then Jess's gaze found his. He tipped his hat and cleared the emotion from his throat. "Gotta go put Slim and Pickens in the barn."

Angie spun in his direction. "I'm helping!"

"Perfect," his mother said. "Keep her out there a while, Beau. We need to handle a few things in the house before we fly the kite. C'mon gang, all hands on deck."

Angie grinned as she walked over to him. "It's balloon blowing time. And I don't hafta do it."

"Not today, sis. And thanks to those pigs, neither do I." He wrapped an arm around her shoulders as they headed back to the corral. "Having a good birthday?"

"The best. The family ride was epic and I loved calling the race for those pigs." She took Pickens' harness and leash off the rail where they'd left them. "I appreciate you letting me."

"You were great at it." He grabbed the ones with Slim's name on them.

"Thank you. By the way, we've all heard the gist of Mom's kite lecture."

"I had a feeling." He held the gate for her and followed her in. "Did you all just pass the word around? Or—"

"Mom sent out a group text. Not to you, obviously." She offered Pickens a treat and put on his harness. "She told us what the situation is with your dad. Since you know, finally, she figured she could inform the rest of us, especially since you might invite him here."

That explained the reactions he'd been getting all day. "I'm sure you have an opinion about it."

"Not about your dad. That's your business. But we've agreed that if you don't propose to Jess sometime soon, you're an idiot."

He smiled. "Isn't that my business, too?"

"Not really. She's having a next-generation McLintock. Besides, we like her. We've voted her onto the island. You just need to make it official."

"I'll take that under advisement."

"Please do." She clipped the leash on Pickens' harness. "We might as well feed them since Mom wants me out of the way."

He chuckled. "And I suppose it has nothing to do with the fact you love watching them eat?"

"I do! They're so cute the way they snort and snuffle. If you ever decide to give away—"

"Not happening. Get your own pigs."

"I just might." After she led Pickens out of the corral, she broke into a slow jog and giggled as Pickens trotted along with her. "Pickens, you're a speedster."

Slim wasn't about to be left behind, so the group made it to the barn in record time. Beau handed Slim's leash to Angie. "If you'll settle them in their stall I'll fetch their food."

"Gotcha."

When he came back with the bowls of chopped veggies, Angie was crouched between two blissed-out pigs lying on their backs as she scratched their tummies. He gave her a mock frown. "You're gonna spoil them."

"Can't. You've already spoiled them. I'll have to watch you like a hawk with that baby or you're liable to spoil my niece or nephew, too."

"Fat chance of that with Jess around."

"Which is why you need to keep her around." She stood and took the bowls of food. "Here you go, piggies."

As they scrambled to their feet and began munching away, Angie joined him outside the stall and leaned against the door to watch. "Adorable."

"If I come out some morning and find them gone, I'll know where to look."

"Yeah, I wouldn't do that. They like me but they *love* you." She gave him a hip bump. "So do I."

"Backatcha, birthday girl."

"Are you gonna invite your dad to visit? I want to meet the guy who sent you all that cool stuff, especially the kite."

"I'm going to ask if he can come in August, toward the middle of the month when the baby's due."

"Awesome! Do you think he still has a contact with whoever made your kite?"

"Don't know."

"I hope so, because I want to buy one. Could be out of my price range, but he might be able to find me a deal since we're sort of related."

"It's worth a try. In the meantime, let's go fly mine. I might consider joint ownership of the kite." Hungry for the sight of Jess, he ushered Angie out of the barn.

* * *

The whirlwind of activities kept Jess from spending much time with Beau. Flying the kite was a family affair, and when it was her turn to hold the spool of kite string, she took over from Cheyenne.

He handed it over carefully. "It's a massive kite. Tugs quite a bit."

"I think I've got it, but you're welcome to stay and make sure I'm solid."

"You're doing fine." He hesitated. "I guess Beau told you about the situation with his dad."

"Yesterday at lunch. I hope to meet the guy in August."

"I hope to meet him, too. My dad, I mean Clint's and mine, comes around every so often, and after I got older I could tell Beau felt weird that his dad never visited. But since he stonewalled us on the subject, we let it go."

"At least now it's out in the open."

"Because of you. And the baby. If that hadn't happened, Beau might still be stuck in his turtle shell."

She glanced at him. "I hadn't thought of it that way."

"The point is, I'm happy about you and the baby being part of the family. We all are."

"Thanks, Cheyenne." She flashed him a smile. "So after the kite flying, what's next?"

"Pretty much a replay of the night you were trapped here by the blizzard. Except with a gazillion balloons, cake and presents after dinner."

"Then poker?"

"Absolutely. Buck and Marybeth will be playing tonight." He grinned. "Hope you brought your A-game again."

"You bet I did."

But by the time she sat down at the poker table, she'd become so fascinated by the change in Beau that she completely lost interest in the game. He wasn't playing well, either, but no one would know from his cheerful expression. He looked as if he'd just won the lottery and hadn't told anyone yet.

The glow of happiness in his eyes and his easy smile had a different quality from his life-of-the-party persona. He laughed often, like the old Beau, only he was letting others tell the jokes instead of taking the stage himself.

For some reason he'd given up being the family's court jester. Whether that was a temporary or permanent change remained to be seen, but it sure added to his appeal. She'd been in love with him for most of her life, but never more than tonight.

He ran out of chips before she did. He didn't buy more.

Buck called down the table. "Beau, you done for the evening?"

"Yes, sir, I am. Just waiting to see how Jess fares in the next hand."

Her breath caught. "Why?"

"Well, in addition to this being Angie's birthday, it's also Valentine's Day. Or more precisely, Valentine's Night. I was thinking we could take a romantic drive, you, me and the little one."

Her pulse shot into the red zone. *Yes, please.* She turned to her dad, who'd claimed the chair on her left. "Want my chips?"

"Sure."

She peered at him. He also looked as if he'd won the lottery and wasn't telling anyone. "Here you go." By the time she'd pushed her chips over, Beau had come around the table to help her out of her chair. She glanced at the group. "Um, see you guys, later. Happy Birthday, Angie."

"Thanks, Jess. The gift card's great. I'm sure I'll use it." Angie's voice sounded funny, like she was holding back either a shout or a laugh. "Beau, don't forget what I said."

"I won't, sis. Happy Birthday. 'Bye, all." A hand at Jess's waist, he ushered her out of the room and down the hallway. Sam followed them until Desiree called him back. A muted *hell, yeah* was followed by shushing noises.

Jess lowered her voice. "A drive?"

"Yes, ma'am. That's accurate." He helped her on with her coat and shoved his arms into his jacket before grabbing his hat. He opened the door.

She shivered in the blast of cold air. "You mean *go for a drive* like set out with no particular destination in mind?"

"I have a destination in mind." Closing the door behind them, he slipped his arm around her waist and tucked her against his side as they crossed the porch and descended the steps. "I'd like to take you home with me, if that's okay."

Cold? What cold? She immediately turned into a one-woman furnace. "That's very okay."

"Just like that? No more questions? Objections?"

"No questions or objections. Spending Valentine's Night with you sounds lovely."

"Well, good, then." He wasted no time getting them both in the truck and on their way. He didn't strike up a conversation as they headed down the road.

She wasn't in the mood to talk, either. But she kept looking at his strong profile in the light from the dash. And every time she did, he turned and looked right back. She had to unbutton her coat or risk overheating.

He parked quickly, helped her out and hustled her over to the house, up the steps and through the front door.

Breathing fast, she blinked once. And gasped. A banner spanned the entire living room. The flowing script used thick red yarn to spell out *WILL YOU MARRY ME?*

She spun around, laughing and crying at the same time. "*Yes!*"

"Thank God." He gathered her close. "I've put you through so much, I wasn't sure if you— I made the sign with strings. Did you see it's strings? That's because—"

"I get it." Tears blurred her vision and she swiped them away. "You're not afraid to be tied down."

"It's even more than that." He cupped her face in both hands. "That whole string phobia was nonsense. I've been yours since our first date."

"Same here, but I didn't think—"

"I just wouldn't admit it. I wasn't going anywhere. Not ever."

She sniffed. "A part of me hoped, but since you never said, I didn't—"

"I kept you guessing. What a jerk. You were right to break up with me, but damn, that hurt."

"It hurt me, too."

"And I'll spend a lifetime making up for that. I love our baby for giving me a second chance." His voice roughened. "I love you, Jess. I love you so much."

"I love you right back, you wonderful man."

"I'm a lucky man, is what I am. Mom said that on Sunday and I wasn't ready to believe her. But slowly it penetrated my thick skull, and by the time I met you for lunch, I knew what I wanted. I just hoped you still wanted me."

"On Monday? You knew you were going to ask me to marry you on *Monday*?"

"Yes, ma'am."

"Why didn't you say so?"

"I wanted to make this banner. That's my best talent, by the way. Making banners."

"It's beautiful."

"I wanted something symbolic to show you that I've thought this through. It's not a knee-jerk response."

'You nailed it."

"And I also wanted to talk with your dad and find out if I had his blessing."

"That's what you were doing in his office?"

"Yes, ma'am. I could have texted him about the party."

"What if he'd had objections?"

"I would've moved heaven and earth to win him over. I never want to drive a wedge between you and your dad."

"So that's why he looked like he was keeping a delicious secret."

"Yeah, your dad doesn't have much of a poker face."

"Neither did you, tonight."

"The closer I got to tapping out, which was my goal, by the way, the more I thought about what I wanted to happen tonight. But why were you losing? Last time you were the champ."

"You distracted me. I've never seen you like that, lit up from within. You looked so happy."

"I've never been this happy." He lowered his mouth to hers. "And I have a hunch I'll be even happier after—"

"We get back to the bedroom?"

"After we've been married for fifty or sixty years." His lips brushed hers. "But the bedroom sounds like a really good idea, too."

"Dad says the years go fast."

"Then we'll make every minute count, beginning with this one."

She hummed with pleasure as his mouth captured hers. Dreams did come true, after all.

* * * * *

Cheyenne McLintock never imagined
volunteering for a bachelor auction would
ignite the flames of desire with Kendall Abbott
in STOKING THE COWBOY'S FIRE, book two in
the Rowdy Ranch series!

* * * * *

New York Times bestselling author Vicki Lewis Thompson's love affair with cowboys started with the Lone Ranger, continued through Maverick, and took a turn south of the border with Zorro. She views cowboys as the Western version of knights in shining armor, rugged men who value honor, honesty and hard work. Fortunately for her, she lives in the Arizona desert, where broad-shouldered, lean-hipped cowboys abound. Blessed with such an abundance of inspiration, she only hopes that she can do them justice.

For more information about this prolific author, visit her website and sign up for her newsletter. She loves connecting with readers.

VickiLewisThompson.com

CPSIA information can be obtained
at www.ICGtesting.com
Printed in the USA
BVHW030819280122
627462BV00003B/84